The Honesty Index

By

Kelly James-Enger

To my mom, who taught me to treasure my friends

Acknowledgments

When I started this novel, I was a new mom of a beautiful baby boy, Ryan. Between parenting and freelancing (writing nonfiction is my day job) and surviving the transition from wanna-be-mom to actual mommy, this novel kept sliding to the bottom of my to-do list. It took literally years to finish the draft, then several more years to rewrite, edit, and finish it, which is evidenced by the fact that my "baby" is now approaching seven years old and has a two-year-old sister, Haley. I promise my next one won't take so long!

While this novel may be called *The Honesty Index*, it's really about friendship. Yes, I love my husband and am always grateful for him. (Thank you, sweetie, for all that you do!) But I am also indebted to a slew of amazing women who have enriched my life in every possible way.

So I thank my mom for all of the obvious reasons; my "old" friends Cindy, Deanne, Hannelore, Laura, and Monica; my many writer friends including Jill, Kris, Polly, Gina, Janine, and Kelly; my "mommy" friends, especially Angie, Katie G, Katie K, Katie M, Lisa, and Valerie; and other special friends and family including GJ, Diana, and "Solid Gold" sista, Stephie. I give special kudos to Sharon for demonstrating great hands-on mommy skills, and to Abby for being not only my much beloved-buddy but my loyal pen pal for nearly a quarter of a century.

And every day I am blessed to know and love two very special women, Jodi and Chaleigh. Without them, I wouldn't be able to answer to the sweetest word I've ever heard—"Mommy."

Chapter 1
Renee

The worst lies are the ones we tell ourselves.
--author Richard Bach

Possibly the only thing worse than lying to yourself is discovering that you have been. That's why most people get very good at denying certain truths to themselves, no matter how obvious, how blatant, or how pronounced they may be. That fact should have comforted Renee. It didn't.

Renee rolled onto her left side, and doubled the pillow under head. It didn't help. Colleen's guestroom pillows were flattened like graham crackers, all of the hospitality squeezed out of them by other unfamiliar heads. The red flannel sheets felt warm and overly intimate against her bare legs. Even when she stretched, searching for a cooler spot, they rubbed against her like a needy dog.

Renee sighed and sat up. She wouldn't be able to get back to sleep. Besides, she could hear Colleen and her kids, a collection of high-pitched voices and Colleen's calmer, lower-pitched one, downstairs in the kitchen.

Renee reached for a pair of striped pull-on pants and tugged them up over her underwear, letting Lars' old gray Wash U T-shirt flop over the waistband.

She stopped in the bathroom to pee, stepping carefully through the slew of bath toys scattered on the fluffy yellow rug, and splashed water over her face. She ignored her reflection. She knew she looked tired. Face it. She looked like crap. But it didn't matter, did it?

Downstairs, Colleen was in the kitchen kneeling next to Taylor, helping her with her backpack. "Did you remember your homework?"

"Yeeessssss! I told you already!" Taylor, Colleen's oldest, pulled away from her mother, rolling her eyes. "I put it in my backpack last night." She shook her head, hands on her non-existent hips.

Colleen looked up at Renee and smiled. "My little type A. Course, if I don't ask, there will be trauma later when she realizes it's still on the kitchen table." She ran a hand over her daughter's silky blond ponytail as Taylor pulled away from her. "Coffee?"

Renee nodded. Colleen pulled a chunky sea-green mug from the cabinet above the sink, pouring a cup from the Krupp's maker on the counter. Forget Folgers. Colleen always had good coffee—she bought it by the bag from Starbucks—and real cream as well.

"Mommy! Mommy, I can't find my socks shirt!" Jordan came thudding into the room, his chubby cheeks flushed. "Mommy!" His voice rose to a wail. "I NEEEEEED it!"

Colleen handed Renee her coffee and turned toward her son just as Rose tossed her bowl of dry Cheerios on the floor from the high chair where she was sitting. She screeched and threw her arms in the air.

Renee closed her eyes, trying to tune out the ruckus, and took a deep swallow of coffee just as the doorbell rang. Rose screeched again, and Taylor dashed out of the kitchen, footsteps pounding on the hardwood floor. Jordan was still wailing about his socks shirts, pulling on

Colleen's sleeve, while Colleen was busily scooping up errant Cheerio's from the floor. "Jordan, take a deep breath! I'll get your shirt in just a minute," said Colleen. She raised her voice. "Taylor! Do you have everything?"

Was every morning like this? Renee was amazed at the noise three relatively small people could make. She pushed herself off of the counter where she'd been trying to stay out of the line of fire, and took the bowl from Colleen. Colleen pushed herself up off the floor with a small noise. "Thanks. Just a sec." As Renee started gathering Cheerio's, Jordan stood next to her crying, snot running from his nose.

"Mo-om! Mom, I am *leaving*!" Taylor yelled. "Right NOW!"

Renee heard Colleen's muffled response, then the slam of the front door.

Colleen returned, rubbing her arms, a piece of clothing in her hand and saw Renee dumping the Cheerio's in the garbage. "Oh, that's okay. You can give them back to her — she's going to throw more of them than she eats, anyway."

Renee shrugged and handed the bowl back to Rose, who snatched it happily, shoving several Cheerio's into her slobbery mouth. Colleen knelt down in front of Jordan, cupping his face in her hand. "Jordy?"

Jordan looked up. His face was red and tear-streaked.

"Look familiar?" Colleen offered him a black and white shirt.

Jordan opened his mouth, grabbed it, and ran upstairs, his meltdown miraculously cured.

"You're welcome!" Colleen called. She looked at Renee. "And he would be the type double-A."

Rose banged her hands down on the high chair, laughing, and the bowl bounced off the top of the chair, launching Cheerio's throughout the air. The bowl and a few pieces of cereal came to rest next to Colleen's foot. Renee sat open-mouthed, but Colleen walked over to Rose's high chair, shaking her head.

"Third time's the charm. That means you are all done, baby girl." In one smooth motion, she wiped the baby's face with a paper towel, pulled her out of the high chair, and set her down on her hands and knees, where she squealed again and began scooting around on all fours. Jordan re-appeared, wearing a White Sox t-shirt (*Sox!* Not *socks!* Duh, thought Renee!) and baggy black sweatpants.

"Did you forget something?"

He squinted at her. "No…huh uh."

"'Thank you, Mommy, for finding my shirt.'" Colleen prompted.

His face brightened as he got it. "Thank you, Mommy, for finding my shirt." He dashed over to his mother and hugged her.

"See how easy that was? All you had to do was ask me to help you find it. You didn't have to have a complete and total meltdown, now, did you?"

He lowered his head, pressing his lips together, and shook his head in agreement. "No." He looked up then, his face still pink with exertion. "But it's my *favorite!*"

Colleen sighed and looked at Renee. "I know, honey," she said, stroking her son's hair. "Get your coat on. It's time for preschool." She looked over at Renee. "Can you keep an eye on the baby? I'll be back in ten minutes. We'll have two hours to ourselves." She gestured to Rose. "More or less."

"Sure thing." Renee listened to them leave, Jordan babbling about something to do with Michael S. and Connor. The door closed behind them, and the house was strangely still after the noise. Renee drank more coffee. The kitchen looked the same as before; a large, sunny room painted bright green. Scribbled pictures in varying colors of crayon hung from the refrigerator, dishes were piled in the sink, and toys, books, little cars, and stuffed animals were scattered over the table and floors. Colleen was no longer the neat freak she'd been when they'd been roommates in college and after. Of course they were always living in cramped quarters—with no children. Colleen's home was a bigger, brighter, louder version of the bungalow she shared with Lars. More space, more stuff, more people…more everything.

Renee drank more coffee, and leaned over to check on Rose, who was happily chewing on the back end of a stuffed rabbit. The rabbit was soaked with drool, as was her chin. She caught Renee's eye and grinned, her lips shiny, and waved the rabbit at her.

By the time Colleen returned, Renee had started on a second cup of coffee and Rose had ditched the rabbit in favor of Renee's pants. She sat between Renee's feet, staring at the different colors of stripes, and occasionally pulling some fabric into her mouth. Renee didn't stop her. The pants were clean, and the baby's warm, meaty hands fondling her ankles felt strangely comforting.

She heard Colleen come in through the back door. "Baby still alive?"

"Yes, and enamored by my pants."

"Come here, drool machine." Colleen bent and scooped her daughter onto her hip, and deposited her on the floor, among a haphazard stack of pillows. "It's time for mother's little helper!" She switched on the television and turned on a DVD. A giraffe puppet bounced across the screen to strains of classical music.

"What is that?"

"Baby Mozart. Puppets, toys, lights, all to Mozart music. Supposed to make them smarter. All I know is they work."

"Watching them makes your kids smarter?"

"Jury's out on that one." Colleen topped off Renee's mug without being asked, and brought her own full mug over to the kitchen table, wiping toast crumbs out of the way. "But they keep them occupied for 27 minutes, and that's saying something."

Renee looked at Rose, who had abandoned her in favor of the television screen, which now featured a red, blue, and yellow toy train. She had pulled one foot into her mouth and drool ran down her ankle.

Colleen poured herself more coffee and settled into a chair across from Renee, pulling her leg up under her. She took a long swallow and sighed. "Okay. All three children accounted for. I'm all yours." She smiled. "And I am happy to see you. I miss you!"

"I know. I miss you, too." Colleen was always after Renee to visit, but the last couple of years she'd been too busy with the mansion. She never expected Colleen to come down to St. Louis—not with the kids and all. She'd come up for a couple of days right after Rose was born, but even that visit had been cut short thanks to a work crisis.

Colleen waved her hand. "It's nobody's fault. I'm just glad you're here. I told Pete we were going out tonight—just you and me. Sound good?"

Renee nodded. She had arrived the night before, but the nearly six-hour drive had left her achy and irritable. The last thing she'd wanted had been to talk. She'd hugged Colleen, promised they'd catch up in the morning, and then crawled into the double bed and fallen asleep within minutes, a respite from the events of earlier in the day. She took a deep breath. "I guess I have some big news."

"Yes?" Colleen leaned forward. "I'm listening."

"You know Lars and I have been talking about getting married for a long time." Renee's voice sounded so calm and neutral to her own ears.

"I know! Like, let's say, years." Colleen was smiling.

Oh boy. Colleen was in for a big shock. "That's why I came up. We're not getting married. Apparently ever."

"What?" Colleen's mouth opened, closed, and

opened again. "What? You're kidding me."

"I'm not kidding."

"But you've been together for four years now!"

"Almost six years." Not that it felt that long to Renee. She looked at Colleen, and almost laughed at her shocked expression. "I know. I'm sorry. I should have given you the heads-up."

"I don't understand! What could have happened after all this time?"

"I don't know, Col. Do you remember he started that business last year—the T-shirt thing. I know he's wanted out of the mansion forever, but it's never worked out that way. So we talked about it, and we agreed that he'd launch this little company, and after he got it off the ground—assuming it got off the ground—we could start making plans. Like set the date. 'Go for it,'" she added. "His words."

"T-shirts?" Colleen poured more cream into her coffee. "I'm sorry. Remind me. Like sports stuff?"

"No, pop culture. He did some that said 'Team Jolie' and 'Team Aniston' last year, but his big sellers are stuff like 'chicks rule' or 'beer: helping ugly people get laid for centuries.'" Renee snorted. "We actually came up with that one together. Classy, huh? Anyway, the company got written up in *The Post-Dispatch* a few months after he started, and sales took off."

"So, what is it? It sounds like he's doing great."

"He is. He's got people on staff now, and he's hoping for sales of half a million this year. I still can't believe how successful it's been."

"Uh huh? I still don't see the problem."

Renee sighed, and put her hands on her face. Then she looked back at her friend. "He says this has made him 'realize his potential,' whatever that means. That this is the first time he's gone after something he wanted, and now he realizes he has no limits. He's already looking into expanding into underwear and shorts with his business." She pulled her dark hair back into a brief ponytail before shaking it out again. "So he's putting all of his time and energy into that. Into the business."

Colleen was silent for a moment. "I still don't understand. He can put his time and energy into his business and still get married."

Renee forced a laugh. "Yeah, I believe I said something very similar. So he changed his story. He said it's not just the business. He loves me, but he doesn't want to get married."

"But you have been talking about it forever…"

"Yes, *talking* about it. But as he explained to me yesterday, he said that talking about it was just that. He was never sure he really wanted to get married, but he assumed that at some point, he'd *know* it was the right time, and he'd do it. Now he knows that there won't be a right time. Because he doesn't want to get married." Renee lifted her coffee cup. "So, that's my big news. Cheers!"

Colleen shook her head. "I'm sorry, Renee. I'm so sorry. What are you going to do?"

"I don't know." Renee's chest felt tight. It hurt to breathe. "Got any ideas?"

"I've got nothing. I'm still in shock."

"Tell me about it." Renee saw Colleen twist her wedding ring without realizing it. Peter and Colleen had been together for almost a decade. That was nearly a third of their lives. Colleen had met Peter, they'd fallen in love, and they'd been engaged within a couple of months. Peter had known that Colleen was the woman he wanted. Renee had assumed they'd follow the same path—even if it took Lars a lot longer to get to their destination.

Renee stood up suddenly and started pacing the kitchen. "I know what you're thinking. You're thinking I should have seen this coming. But I didn't. I really didn't. I was happy for him! I was happy he'd finally found something he was going to stick with." She grabbed the back of one of the kitchen chairs. "And of course I helped him get the business off the ground." She forced a smile. "Because I'm such a wonderful, loving, helpful *girlfriend.*" She emphasized the last word.

Colleen didn't say anything, just waved her hand, encouraging her to continue.

"So, I pretty much feel like a gigantic idiot. All this time I have believed in us. Who cares if we weren't married? I knew we'd get married eventually. I knew he wasn't ready. No problem. I can wait! Then I started working at the mansion, and I kept waiting. And then it didn't really seem to matter. We may as well be married, as far as his family is concerned." She swallowed hard again. "But you and I know it's not the same thing. Is it wrong to want that commitment? Why can't I just accept things the way they are?"

"Well, maybe you can," Colleen said reasonably. "Can't you go on living together? You've been happy, haven't you?"

"Yeah." Renee felt tears come to her eyes. "Yeah. We have been."

"So..."

"I want more than that," said Renee. "I want him to want what I want too."

"Makes total sense to me."

"So why do I feel so pathetic and needy and like I'm a personal insult to feminists everywhere? Why can't I just be happy with what I have?"

"You want me to be honest?"

"Yeah."

"Because you want more than he does, Renee. And if you want to get married and he doesn't, someone is going to have to settle. Other than having a child, I can't imagine a more major impasse." Colleen glanced over at Rose, who was still transfixed by the television. "Actually, that would be a more major impasse. If one person wants a child and the other one doesn't, well, that's worse. Parenthood is a permanent thing."

Renee pulled her hair away from her face. "I thought he and I were a permanent thing." Renee's mouth twisted, and she took a tissue from Colleen's outstretched hand. "I'm an idiot."

"Stop. You're in love. That's not idiocy. That's life."

"Well, my life is now a huge screwed-up mess. Let's see. We live together. I work for his family. I spend all my time with his family." She ticked things off on her fingers. "And oh yeah, I'm in love with a man who doesn't love me enough to marry me." Her voice broke. "Yeah, this coming year is looking great."

"Well, what does his mom say?" Colleen knew how close Renee and Mollie were. "She loves you!"

"I know. We don't talk about him that much, though. I don't know if she's thrilled about Speak Up taking off—she still wants him to buy into the mansion—but on the other hand, he's her son. She wants him to be happy."

"But you make him happy."

"Or have made him happy."

"So, what are you going to do?" That was Colleen, always cutting to the heart of the issue. Renee still was hoping that she'd have some kind of plan.

"I don't know. I told Mollie yesterday I needed some time off," said Renee. A thought suddenly flashed through her mind. "Maybe I'm wrong about her being clueless. Mollie must know something because she didn't even ask me why I was taking the time." She shook her head. "I still can't believe this is happening. Lars is—he's my whole life."

Renee stopped, remembering the fortune cookie she'd opened the day before meeting Lars. "You are about to embark on a delightful journey." And then she'd met him at the mansion the next night, with no clue that he was the son of the owners.

It had been a sign—and there had been plenty of others, too. Favorite song? Pink Floyd, *Wish you Were Here*. Favorite food? Pasta arrabiata, with loads of olive oil and flecks of red pepper that singed your tongue. At night he still slept with an arm thrown over her, even after all this time. His family had become hers. They'd worked together, cooked together, fixed up their (okay, his) little bungalow together.

Maybe she'd been a little suspicious of her good fortune at first, and tried to keep herself from getting too enmeshed. But you can only keep your heart caged and your dreams locked up for so long. Less than two months after she'd met him, she'd known that she loved him, and then she fell in love with his family too. Then it was easy. Loving him was as thoughtless as breathing. Even now. Especially now.

Chapter 2
Colleen

Colleen smiled at the bartender, a tall, skinny man in his mid-fifties. "Can I get a Vodka Collins, please?" She slung her purse over the barstool, grimacing as she felt a brief flash of pain in her shoulder. "Renee?"

"Let me think." Renee stared at the bottles behind the bar. "Oh, I don't care." She turned to the bartender. "Can I just get a glass of the house white?" She turned to Colleen. "I like this place. Kind of reminds me of the Hill," said Renee, shifting on her barstool to scan the room. "How's the food?"

"It's no Charlie Gitto's, but it's good," said Colleen. "And I love the vibe here." The room was dim but not dark, with burgundy-shaded table lamps dotting the bar. The wall behind the bottles was smoky glass that reflected the hundred or so bottles of spirits lined up on shelves. Several couples sat at tall, round tables near the bar. Dean Martin crooned *Volare* over the muted noise of conversation and silverware on china coming from the restaurant through the doors to the bar. Colleen gestured at the glasses the bartender had set in front of them. "And they make big drinks."

Renee glanced at the wine glass without comment. She picked it up by the stem to clink it against Colleen's.

"To friendship," prompted Colleen. "And to a new year."

Renee nodded, and took a small sip of wine. Colleen took a deeper swallow of hers. The drink was just how she liked it—strong, but mellowed by the sweetness of the mix. She reminded herself not to drain it all in one gulp. Renee had enough trauma going on. She didn't need her best friend getting drunk.

Not that I get drunk, Colleen corrected herself. I just get...lubricated. Socially lubricated, as Pete would say. After a day of dealing with diapers and meltdowns and power struggles and laundry and the endless feeding of children, she looked forward to that drink. Maybe a little too much, but she wouldn't be the first mom whose Mother's Little Helper was a big glass of chardonnay.

Within a few minutes, Colleen felt that familiar unloosening, the slight slackening of her body, a warmth expanding over her face. She stretched back, took a deep breath, and stretched her neck. Better.

She wasn't surprised that Renee had barely touched her wine. Even in college, she could nurse a drink all night. Unlike most of the other girls in the dorm (including herself), Renee had never splashed vomit in the communal bathroom due to overconsumption of alcohol. Of course now she knew why.

"I'm sorry?"

Renee nodded over her shoulder at a pair of men in their early 40s who were sliding onto barstools a few seats away. "That guy waved at you."

Colleen raised her hand in greeting. To Renee, she said, "The guy on the left, Roger, he lives a couple of blocks away from us. He's got a son in Taylor's class."

Renee nodded, uninterested. "So? Have you come up with a plan for me?"

The question was teasing, her tone anything but. Renee looked tired, Colleen realized—not mom-tired, which was a whole different universe of beyond-bone-weary exhaustion, but just spent. And sad. Which made sense, after all. She couldn't imagine Pete coming home and telling her he didn't want to be married anymore. That was the stuff of *Lifetime* movies and nightmares—stuff that didn't happen, at least not to anyone she knew. "I don't know, Renee. Even if you leave, would you still work for his mom?"

Renee twirled the wine in her glass. "I could. But do I want to?" She took a miniscule sip of wine and sighed.

Colleen looked at her friend. "You had *no* idea?" It seemed like Renee should been able to sense something was off. There must have been some clue, some signal of an impending crash that she had missed. Or denied.

"I suppose I *should* have had some idea. I mean, I realize objectively that if we've been together this long and we're still not married, there's your clue, right?" Renee took a sudden gulp of her wine.

Colleen had privately thought the same thing for years, and had even shared it with Pete. Now was not the time to drop that particular bomb. "Don't beat yourself up. *He's* the one with the problem," she added.

"I guess. But that just makes me the one in love with the one with the problem."

Colleen tried to switch gears. "Have you said anything to your mom?"

Renee made a face. "God, no. She'll take it hard. She *loves* Lars. Of course her advice to me was if I wanted to get married so bad, I should just get pregnant."

Colleen stared at her, unsure of what to say.

"No." Renee raised her hand. "Trust me, I didn't take her advice. That really *was* an accident."

Colleen reached over and put her arm around her friend. "I'm sorry, sweetie."

Renee excused herself to go to the bathroom, and Colleen let her go. Renee didn't like big emotional scenes;

in college, she had strived for an air of ironic detachment. Colleen had been a little scared when she met her freshman roommate for the first time. Renee had come sidling into the room, a giant army backpack over one shoulder, her shaggy black hair (dyed, Colleen later learned) falling over one eye. Colleen had immediately started planning to ask for a change of roommate. What had she been thinking?

Yet they'd clicked right away. Renee called it the proximity factor—they spent so many hours in their tiny box of a dorm room, after all—but it was more than that. On the outside, they hadn't had much in common. Maybe nothing. Renee's wardrobe consisted of skinny black jeans, Cure T-shirts, and lace-up sneakers that made her look even younger than she was. She listened to music Colleen had never heard of and her hands were often stained with ink, paint, or chalk, depending on what she was working on. But Renee's look was only that, Colleen had quickly discovered—a look. Somewhere in high school she'd decided she might as well embrace the outsider uniform, and she'd done so. By the time they'd graduated from school, Colleen had gotten Renee wearing colors other than black—even if that was her default setting.

Renee settled back on the barstool next to her, giving her a brief smile. "Sorry."

"You never have to apologize to me," Colleen glanced at the bartender and he caught her glance and brought her another drink. She'd make this the last one; she was driving, after all.

"Col, do you mind if I stay another day or two? Do you have any plans or anything?"

Colleen felt a tiny sting. Plans? What kind of plans did Renee mean? They'd spent the entire day together. Let's see, the baby had been fed five times, changed seven, coddled into a nap twice. Jordan had been dropped off and picked up from preschool, and then entertained his best friend Connor all afternoon. Taylor had come home in tears because Sasha had said she wanted to be Madison's best friend now, not Taylor's. Colleen had made a mental note to throttle Sasha, who strung Taylor along like a commitment-phobic bachelor. Taylor could zoom from Sasha's "BFF" to the second-grade version of dog poop in the course of a day, and just as quickly back. But she insisted Sasha was her Very Best Friend Forever, no matter what. Then Colleen had made dinner for the kids (macaroni and cheese, with cut-up hot dogs—nauseating for adults but delicious for pre-puberty children), overseen quick baths, hustled them into their pajamas, and put the baby down just before Pete had come home. Then she'd made a quick dinner for the grownups—pasta with spinach, feta cheese, and olive oil with a side salad—and cleaned up the kitchen. And Renee? Well, she had moped around, flipping through magazines, occasionally playing with the baby. She was a guest, of course, but she hadn't offered to help—other than carrying the dirty dishes to the sink.

Colleen kept her voice light. "Oh, let's see. Tomorrow's itinerary includes a trip to the grocery store, followed by a run to the dry cleaners and possibly a delightful meal at McDonald's Play Place."

"Oh, okay." Renee's voice was disinterested. Whether it was disinterest in Colleen's day, Colleen's life, or everything in general, Colleen couldn't tell.

"Sorry!" Colleen said, forcing a laugh. "You've seen what *I* do all day. Feed, entertain, hug, soothe, change, pacify, discipline. And repeat. Every day is pretty much the same as every other. So those are the *plans*."

Renee must have caught her tone. "I just don't want to get in your way or anything. I know you weren't planning on me showing up on your doorstep out of the blue."

Colleen immediately felt guilty. "Don't be stupid.

I'm glad you showed up on my doorstep. Even if the circumstances stink."

"Yeah." Renee glanced at her. "Ready to set me straight? I can't help thinking if I'm gone, physically gone, he'll rethink, you know?" She twisted her mouth into a half-smile. "'You don't know what you got until it's gone.' Think there's any truth to that?"

"It's possible." "Out of sight, out of mind," thought Colleen, was just as likely a conclusion. Colleen liked Lars but she had never seen him as marriage material. From what she could see, his status as the only boy (and clearly his parents' favorite) meant he'd grown up in a charmed world. He'd dropped out of school and spent years screwing around, working weekends at the mansion, while his parents had continued paying his rent! She'd been shocked when Renee had told her that—and a little jealous. Where were Colleen's rich relatives? Still, she could understand Lars' appeal. He was good-looking in his Nordic kind of way, laid-back, and he had a natural ease with people, a charisma. But charisma and staying power rarely came in the same package.

"And if nothing changes? What then?" Colleen asked. She realized that if Renee didn't go back to St. Louis, she could go anywhere. She could start over. Renee could pick up and move anywhere she wanted. Forget St. Louis—she could live in the city like she and Pete had when they first moved here. Forget Lincoln Park, which had grown too expensive—now neighborhoods like Wicker Park and Roscoe Village were the up-and-coming places to live.

And Renee didn't even have to stay in Chicago! She really could go anywhere. She didn't have to worry about anyone but herself. Cutting Lars loose could wind up being the best thing for Renee in the long run. But she'd have to figure that out for herself.

Chapter 3
Renee

Renee was just getting dressed when her cell phone chirped. She picked it up automatically, forgetting for a moment that there was no one she wanted to talk to.

"This is Betty Ridgely, Renee. I'm calling about our anniversary party. I've decided to make some changes to the menu."

Renee located her mental picture of Betty Ridgely, a taut-faced 50-something blonde with the pinched look of someone who has never had as much to eat as she would like. Betty was your prototype Ladue lady who lunched, did Pilates, played golf, dieted, volunteered, and planned expensive soirees featuring fattening exotic foods she then abstemiously ignored. Ladue Ladies comprised a good portion of her clients at the mansion. Who else but the residents of expensive suburbs like Ladue and Clayton could afford to rent the elegant nineteenth-century former home complete with nine working fireplaces, seating for up to 200, and a menu limited only by her imagination and her client's bank account?

"Mrs. Ridgely, I'm actually away from the mansion at the moment." She didn't say she was out of state (even out of town), or that at the present moment she had no idea whether she would ever return to the mansion. That seemed like a lot for her client to handle all at once. It certainly was for her.

"Well, you certainly can still help me with this." Betty's voice was cool but certain. And why not? She had changed her mind about the party a half-dozen times already. First she wanted white-gloved waiters. Then that was passé. Originally she had opted for a sit-down dinner—then she switched it to a fusion menu consisting of hot and cold hors d'oeuvres. She'd refused to listen to Renee's wine suggestions, insisting that she had a personal friend who was a sommelier to help her make the appropriate choices. Based on the calls she'd made and the extent of the various seating arrangements and menu alterations, Renee guessed she was putting more time into the party than she had her wedding. So they'd been married thirty years. So what?

"I suppose you think I'm ridiculous making all these changes," said Betty, as if reading her mind. She sighed. "I've hosted dozens of parties over the years. I've even chaired charity events! I'm driving *myself* crazy. And Harold." She paused. "But this is an important date for us. "Harold had prostate cancer last year and...we thought...we thought...well, we were lucky. Incredibly lucky. And we—well, I—want everything to be simply perfect."

Great. Renee had been harboring endless resentment at her unreasonable requests, and the woman's husband had nearly died. Now she could feel guilty for her lack of compassion on top of everything else. Of course it was a big day for her.

Renee dropped her soothing-client voice and spoke in her normal tone. "I'm glad to hear he's doing well now, Mrs. Ridgely," she said. "And I understand that you want everything to be perfect. It will be, I promise you. May I suggest that you speak with Mollie, though, as I'm away from the mansion? If you call her anytime after 9 a.m., she'll be able to help you." She made a mental note to send Mollie a quick email giving her a heads-up.

"Mollie? Oh, she was delightful. That's fine. I'll call her," said Betty. "Thank you, Renee."

Renee hung up, surprised at the warmth in Betty's tone. Maybe she'd overreacted to her demands. She'd been doing that lately, and no wonder. Years of planning other people's parties, fetes, soirees, fundraisers, showers, weddings, reunions, and brunches had worn her down. She was close to the point of not caring whether the spray of calla lilies in the second lounge was fresh, or whether the servers' black uniforms (Mollie insisted on uniforms, saying it added to the sense and elegance of the place) were neatly pressed, or whether the chipotle pork quichelettes were flaky enough and served. Every event required orchestrating a million niggling little details. Screw up one, just one, and the client complained.

Then again, she usually didn't screw up. She had a decent memory, and an innate sense for design. Her tables, she knew, were gorgeous, and she'd learned the difference between a pinot gris and a chardonnay, Brie and Camembert, and knew why sushi-grade tuna tasted different than the kind she had always eaten—you know, the kind that came in a can with a smiling fish on it.

She'd learned, and Mollie had gradually given her more responsibility, letting her take over small events—luncheons, showers, intimate cocktail parties—at first. Now she and Mollie divided the events, with Renee covering most of the weekend ones. Renee didn't mind. Most of the time Lars was working there for big parties anyway—either helping in the kitchen or parking cars or floating wherever she needed him—so it wasn't like she was missing out on time with him. And there was a certain satisfaction in witnessing an event that unfurled just as she had planned it.

What now, though? The job had seemed like such a

great idea at the time. She wanted out of her office job. Administrative assistant, even for a nonprofit, was just another word for wage slave. She'd worked in restaurants in high school and college, so she had basic hospitality experience. She'd liked Lars' mother, Mollie, immediately. In a matter of weeks, she had become not only a boss, but a second mother—or rather, a better mother, the one she wished for but hadn't had. But the connection—the job, the sense of family, the future she'd assumed—all stemmed from Lars. Take him out of the equation and what did she have?

She'd lived with him long enough to know how slowly he moved, how he made decisions only after months of careful consideration. She knew his gestures, the way he deliberately looked away when someone in his family annoyed him, the smallest twisted smile on his face; the way he steered a guest who had too much to drink gently away by placing his hand on the person's back. Before he started a project at home—the little bungalow always needed some kind of TLC—he'd spend hours looking it over, walking the space with his hands in his pockets, humming under his breath. He'd nearly driven her crazy when they remodeled the kitchen last year. He walked the room, humming and muttering, for the better part of a weekend, stopping occasionally to take measurements and jot them down in a little notebook.

Renee had been ready to start—it was a rare weekend off for her and she wanted to take advantage of the time. "What are you doing?" she finally exploded. "You've been pacing around for hours!"

He had just continued staring at the beaten-looking cabinets above the sink. "I'm making my plan, sweets. Making my plan."

Once he'd decided on his course of action, he worked steadily. They'd chosen new cabinets and flooring—a light pine Pergo she loved—and had laid it over the course of a day. She'd helped him measure and hang the new cabinets, the same stain as the floor, and had returned to find that he'd surprised her with a stainless refrigerator and stove. He'd added a tile backsplash above the sink, with sea blue tiles.

"Well? You like?" He'd gestured around the kitchen with a grin. "I figured might as well spring for the whole nine yards. I picked them last week and they got delivered today."

"They're gorgeous. I love them," she'd said, sliding her hand down the slick coolness of the refrigerator door. And she did. They were no doubt exactly what she would have chosen herself—if she had had the opportunity to choose.

She hadn't brought it up, though. He'd just asked whether she liked them. She did. "So what exactly is the problem, then?" She could see him, standing patiently, his arms at his sides. He never crossed his arms over his chest in a dispute—his mother had told him it looked defensive. Grow up in a family that makes people happy for a living, and you learn a whole different set of manners.

"You should have asked me first. This is my house too." That's what she should have said. But she didn't. Why rock the boat over something insignificant? That's what she had told herself.

Later that morning, after Colleen picked Jordan up from preschool, Renee tagged along with them and the baby to run errands. Their last stop was a strange grocery store. Coconuts hung by the door; a dozen nautical flags dangled from the ceiling. Jordan pulled away from the three of them, jumping on the pad to open the sliding door. "Look, Mommy! I'm opening the door!"

Colleen pulled a cart out and slid Rose into the child seat, unzipping her snowsuit and buckling a strap around her padded, chubby stomach. A woman in her early 20s, sleek blond hair pulled back in a French braid smiled at them. "Hey there! Welcome back to Dealin' Dave's!" She wore jeans, a long-sleeved white shirt, and a brown and red flowered vest. "Can I help you find anything?"

"Balloons!" crowed Jordan, leaping into the air.

"That OK with you, Mom?" said the employee, looking to Colleen. Why not me, thought Renee? I could be his mother, couldn't I?

Colleen nodded, scanning the store, and the woman reached out her hand. "Come on, then! What color do you want?"

Renee could hear him debating as they scampered off. She stared at her friend. "*You* are just letting a stranger run off with your child?"

"She's not a stranger. We're in here every week," said Colleen, picking up a bag of baby spinach. "Her name is Angel, I think."

"What is this place?" Renee hadn't seen a store like it. Huge colorful signs cried, "Organic!" "All-natural!" "Good for you—and your wallet!" and an entire wall bulged with every imaginable supplement from vitamin b-6 to coenzyme Q10 to chewable calcium tablets. Stacks of organic bananas were piled next to bags of apples, and to her right was a huge selection of nuts.

"Whole cashews. Half cashews. Low-salt cashews. Whole *and* half cashews. Jalapeno cashews," read Renee, lifting various bags of cashews. "And that's just the cashews! Look at this! There are walnuts, almonds, pistachios, Brazil nuts, sunflower seeds, soy nuts—wait, what are soy nuts?" Apparently her knowledge of food was lacking an essential element.

"They're soybeans. Those have been roasted and salted," said Angel, who appeared at her shoulder, Jordan tagging behind her with a blue balloon tied to one wrist, a purple one tied to the other. "They're yummy. Want me to open a bag so you can try?"

"Ummm, no, that's okay," said Renee. "I was just

wondering."

"Mommy, look! I got two!" Jordan flailed his arms back and forth, making the helium balloons bounce. "Two!"

"And what do you say?" prompted Colleen.

He thought for a moment. "Thank you very much," he said, carefully pronouncing each syllable.

"You're welcome," said Angel, tousling his hair. "He's such a cutie."

"Thanks," said Colleen, smiling. "Hey, did you guys get those frozen meatballs in? Last time, you were out."

"Sure do. I'll grab them for you. How many bags?"

"Two will do it."

"Be right back!" Angel strode off, her braid swishing merrily.

"What's she eating for breakfast?"

"What?"

"She's just so…chipper, that's all."

Colleen leaned over to grab a package of whole-grain bread and set it in the cart. "Jordan, why don't you pick out some fruit roll-ups? You can get ten of them. Can you count that many?"

"Okay!" He dashed over to the bananas, his winter coat and balloons jerking behind him, and dropped to his knees, sorting through boxes of fruit rollups.

"Smart to put them near the floor like that," said Renee, gesturing at the roll-ups.

"Yeah, I love this place. They've got great produce, and all kinds of cereal and crackers and cheap wine, you name it. The people who work here are great."

Angel returned, handing the frozen meatballs to Colleen. "Can I help you find anything else?"

"No, we're good. Thanks, though," said Colleen.

"All righty then! Have a fantastic day!" She smiled and started to pull out bags of walnuts from an open box on a wheeled cart.

Renee selected several cheeses, surprised to note that they had everything from Camembert, to Gouda, Havarti, four brands of Brie, and even blue Castello. The guy in the wine section actually knew that a Bordeaux only came from France and that a pinot gris and a pinot grigio were the same thing.

"I like this place," said Renee, as they stood in line.

"Isn't it fab? One of my neighbors told me about this place, and I can't live without it. Even Pete is addicted to their meatballs. I've even thought I should work here for the employee discount!" Colleen smiled at the guy with glasses behind the register who nodded and started ringing up their groceries.

"What would you do with the kids?"

"Yeah, well, that's the problem," said Colleen, quickly looking away. "I'd have to pay a sitter more than I made, I'm sure."

Renee sensed she'd stumbled onto something painful. "It would be good to get out of the house, though, wouldn't it?"

"Sure. But I don't see that happening at this point," said Colleen. "Besides," she continued, bending to zip up Jordan's coat, "the kids need me at home right now."

Renee dropped the subject. There seemed more to this, but she wasn't sure how to proceed. There was a distance between the two of them that hadn't been there before. She'd noticed it last night at the bar. Renee had been ready to talk, but Colleen had been abrupt, even a bit cold.

Colleen was her oldest friend—they'd bonded as roommates at Southern their freshman year. Renee hadn't expected to like her. Colleen was pretty in the way guys noticed—round blue eyes, shiny blond hair, big boobs—and she'd been a member of just about any club you could belong to in high school. Next to her, Renee felt like a scrawny mutant, barely a female. But when they'd discovered that they had both grown up in tiny farm towns, they'd clicked.

After all, they had both leapt from the known to the unknown, and the unknown was so much bigger than what they were used to. It seemed like everyone Renee met had more money than her, more life experience, and assuredly more confidence. Colleen may have been a cheerleader with a tight gang of high school friends at home, but at school she was just another small-town rube. Or so she confessed to Renee. Renee had expected that college would be a place for her to start over—no more being the weird girl who spent all of her time sketching and reading—but found she felt just as isolated at college as she had in high school, even if she'd escaped the baggage of her mom.

Would they have been friends otherwise? Of course not. College had a way of creating friendships through proximity, but those relationships didn't always survive post-graduation. Theirs had, though—another surprise.

Colleen had graduated with a degree in finance and did the power-suit and pumps thing, working at a big bank in downtown St. Louis. Renee had worked for the nonprofit, hoping to be even a small cog in the wheel of something important. They'd gotten an apartment in Soulard, and spent most of their relatively meager paychecks on meals out. They'd talked about buying a place together—think of what they could save on rent—but then Colleen had met Peter at a bar down the street from their little two-bedroom apartment. In a matter of months, Colleen had fallen in love, gotten engaged, gotten married, and moved away to Chicago—and then just as fast, started having kids.

Renee had tried to make the most of her suddenly empty evenings and weekends. She'd always had a gift for drawing (hey, she'd majored in art for a reason!), and had developed a line of cards that were comic takeoffs of the great works of art. Mona Lisa solemnly giving the finger. Christ and the apostles of the last supper wearing St. Louis Cardinal jerseys and downing pizza and beer. Munch's miserable soul from *The Scream* with a delighted grin and a handful of balloons.

She'd spent more than a year sketching out ideas, finalizing the line, choosing card stock, developing the final prints, and looking for distributors. She'd carried her cards to every card, book, and specialty store she could imagine, only to be told no, no, no. Eventually she gave up. So she wouldn't be a full-time artist. She could still draw for herself, after all. Then her office holiday party had landed her in the mansion, where she'd met Lars. Several months later, Mollie had offered her a job, starting out as her assistant. Now she had a decent salary and even a title to her name. "Special events manager" sounded more impressive than it was in reality but Mollie had started making noises about her buying in to the family business.

"You already are family, of course," Mollie had said six months back. "This would make it official as far as the mansion goes. After all this time, Gene and I are starting to make plans for the future. We'd love to have you and Lars take it over. We'd have to consider the girls, of course, but you know what it takes to keep it running."

But Lars had balked when she'd mentioned it. "Us buy *them* out? Are you joking me? Forget that. I'd be trapped for life!"

Renee had assumed he'd been referring to the mansion. She knew he didn't share the same affection for it his parents and sisters did. To Lars, the mansion wasn't a legacy. It wasn't even a tradition worth keeping. It was work. It was the way his parents had chosen to pay the bills, nothing more. She'd known that. Now it occurred to her that his emotional response to the idea might not have been about the mansion at all. Maybe it had to do with her.

Chapter 4
Colleen

She was three for three. The baby was down, hopefully for the night, Jordan had drifted off during yet one more reading of *Where the Wild Things Are* and even Taylor had succumbed without the usual hassle. The television was on, and Pete was sitting at the kitchen table, eating cold pasta with the newspaper spread out before him, when she came downstairs.

She flopped down in a chair next to him. "They're all down," said Colleen, reaching for a piece of his garlic bread. "You like the sauce?"

He made a thumbs-up sign. "Where's Renee? She finally go home?" He took another bite of pasta and sauce without raising his head from the paper.

She didn't answer.

"Huh? She leave?"

Colleen still didn't answer.

Finally he looked up to see her sitting with her arms folded, looking at him. "What?" He grimaced. "Oh yeah. I forgot. The half-assed conversation." He folded the paper and set it aside, leaning over to give her a brief kiss.

"How was your day, my darling? Is there anything you'd like to talk to me about? What can I do to make my beautiful, amazing wife happy?"

She shoved him gently. "Knock it off. All I ask for is some eye contact. We don't have to have a couples bonding session every night."

"Oh, thank Christ!" he grinned at her, his wide-set eyes narrowing slightly. "Seriously. She take off?"

"No, she said she was going to a movie. I think she was trying to give us a little privacy." She opened the refrigerator and poured herself a glass of merlot, sitting back down. "Like that matters."

He squeezed her hand. "Bad day? I thought you liked having her here."

"I do. But it feels like our friendship...like we're not as close as we were before," said Colleen, sipping her wine. "It's bad enough when you feel misunderstood by people you hardly know. I shouldn't have to explain myself to her. She should *get* me, you know what I mean?"

"I get you," he said, pushing his empty plate aside.

"I know." She picked up his plate and set it in the dishwasher. "But I need friends, too. Or at least one friend," she amended.

"Why don't you say something to her?"

She lifted her finger at him.

"Oh, was I problem-solving when I was simply supposed to listen," he said, crossing his arms. "Sorry 'bout that. Must have misplaced my script."

"Oh, hush." She slid her chair closer to him under the table, snaking her foot up his pant leg. "As long as we have some privacy, want to take advantage of it?" The wine helped. Besides, it seemed like months since he'd held her.

"What's got into you?" He looked at her closely, giving her his full attention. He had lines across his forehead and his hair wasn't as thick as it had once been, but his dark, watchful eyes never changed.

"Does it matter?" She stood, and reached for his hand. "Come on. Let's go get this over with."

He followed her up the stairs. "Not exactly the come-on of my dreams, but I'm a man, right?" he said, teasing her.

Less than ten minutes later, they were lying next to each other, post-orgasmic and relaxed if not truly blissful. "Utility screwing," Pete called these encounters. The sex was purposeful. It wasn't exactly perfunctory, but wasn't the stuff of bodice-rippers, either. At least they still had sex—listening to some of the other moms she knew, sexless marriages were becoming the norm of late. Ironic considering that sex made babies, who then destroyed sex. At least that's what had happened to her.

Taylor had been a colicky baby who had fought sleep with every infant molecule in her body, and it seemed like it was only a matter of months after she finally started sleeping through the night more or less soundly, that Jordan had arrived. Once again, their sex life had taken a predictable but no less depressing nosedive. But they hadn't given it up entirely—and Rose was the unintended result of one night when she was too lazy to get up and put in her diaphragm. Now sex was just about the last thing on her list, something she made an effort to do, not something she truly *wanted* to do. That fact alone was depressing when she stopped to think about it.

"Remember PK?" said Peter. He must be thinking along similar lines.

"Barely." "PK" was their code for pre-kids. She rolled closer to him, pushing her hair behind her ear. "We slept a lot, right?"

"And we screwed constantly! Sometimes for hours. At least I think I remember that," his voice was thick and slow, and he stroked his fingers up her back, tickling her lightly the way she liked.

She leaned onto his chest so she could see his face. "For real? Are you sure?"

He shifted, and she could feel his breath slowing.

He'd be asleep in a few minutes. PK, she would have been out before he was, but insomnia had been the unexpected accompaniment of motherhood. Exhausted as she was, she couldn't fall asleep — or she woke at three in the morning with a start, unable to let her body soften back into slumber. The rare nights she slept soundly were a blessing — and if none of the kids were up all night, bliss unlike anything she could imagine was all hers. She fantasized about sleep the way other women fantasized about chocolate or sex or gourmet kitchens and she often found herself conjuring up delicious images of the perfect pillow-top mattress outfitted with 440-thread count Egyptian cotton sheets and a plethora of fat goose-down pillows, the utter impermeable quiet, the unbreakable peace.

When she was expecting Taylor, she'd lie there dreaming about a sweet, shy boy with her coloring and Peter's wide-set eyes and generous mouth. Instead she'd gotten a red-faced, blond-curled dictator who'd been calling the shots since she arrived after only four hours of labor, fist first, howling all the way.

It hadn't been love at first sight. The first feeling she'd had was denial. That is not *my* baby!

"That was a short labor for a first-time mommy," a nurse had said, efficiently checking her pulse as her doctor stitched her up. Thank God she had opted for an epidural. She couldn't imagine making it through labor otherwise. "Your little girl couldn't wait to meet you."

And then she had looked at the angry infant in her arms and felt a pull of recognition that swallowed any disappointment. This is my baby. My daughter. Her heart had actually hurt at the emotion that had swamped her. It was more than love. It was as if the feelings she'd had for Pete were suddenly insignificant. This was the real thing. Sure, she had been excited about being pregnant, about having a baby. But this wasn't just a fuzzy picture on an ultrasound or the source of those late-night kicks and pokes and heartburn. This was the person she'd been waiting for.

That first night in the hospital, she hadn't slept. She had stayed awake all night, staring at her, stroking her tiny downy cheeks, kissing her tiny tightly clenched fists. She saw Pete in her already, in the shape of her nose and chin, but her ears, at least, were all Colleen's. The night nurse tried to coax her to sleep, telling her she had all the time in the world to admire her new baby. Colleen had waved her off, high on post-delivery endorphins and pregnancy hormones.

She'd planned on going back to work, but she couldn't make herself do it. She had become the woman she never expected, the "career girl" who'd tossed aside her education, salary, benefits, and potential to stay home with her kids. Pete was surprised but fine with her decision to ditch her marketing career in favor of seven pounds, nine ounces of their shared genes. The seven pounds, nine ounces carried a weight that nothing before ever had.

Taylor hit every milestone ahead of time, and Colleen and Pete agreed she was brilliant. Strong-willed, certainly, but who wanted a wallflower? "Knows what she wants and is gonna get it," Pete would say. Other than the constant exhaustion, Colleen was happier than she'd ever been. When Taylor beamed at her with a wide-open, gummy smile, or laughed her deep belly laugh, Colleen would think, "This is it. This is what I was meant to do."

It wasn't until she had Jordan that everything started to fall apart. Jordan was a sweet, complacent baby who rarely cried—the baby Colleen had pictured during her first pregnancy. Now she had the two kids she and Pete had agreed on—a boy and a girl! What could have been any more perfect? She had fantasized about long walks to the park with her double stroller, Taylor bonding with her new baby brother, the four of them cuddling in their king-sized bed on weekends.

Taylor sensed that the world was changing under her feet, and she resented her new brother, disgusted at the idea that she'd have to share the spotlight—not to mention Mommy and Daddy's attention—with anyone, much less a shapeless lump who was always in Mommy's arms. The novelty of "your new baby brother" wore off fast, and she reverted back to baby talk and using diapers, and constantly begged to be held. It was a rough transition. Colleen had thought two kids would equal two times as much work. Instead it seemed like four times as much, maybe five. Though how could she even keep track anymore?

That had to be why she had started fantasizing about going back to work. She didn't say anything to Pete or her mom, but she did tell Renee. Then Renee hadn't understood. "So get a sitter," she'd said. "Or you could put them in daycare, right?"

No, she couldn't put them in daycare. What kind of mom would she be if she did that? Besides, staying home with them was more important, she reminded herself. They would only be little once. And she had wanted to stay home! What was wrong with her?

And it had worked out all right. Between the Y and preschool and play dates and the inevitable trips to McDonalds, the days passed more quickly than she would have expected. Taylor started kindergarten and Jordan was in two-year-olds preschool three mornings a week. Then she was in first grade, Jordan was three, and Colleen realized in just two years, she *could* go back to work. She started updating her resume, hired a sitter, and had a chatty, friendly dinner with several of her former coworkers. She didn't feel as out of the loop as she'd expected, and realized her mind hadn't gone completely soft. Who knew, maybe she could even get hired back at her old firm.

Then one morning the smell of coffee made her gag. She didn't even bother with a pregnancy test. She simply shoved all her grownup clothes in the back of the closet, and vowed to embrace fulltime motherhood for another oh, five or six years. Her career could wait. She already had a job. The most important job in the world.

Chapter 5
Renee

"I'd like an application, please?" Renee stood at the front counter of Dealin' Dave's, feeling ridiculous. The teenager at the register closest to her had purple striped hair and at least seven earrings on one ear alone. I'm not young enough or anywhere cool enough to work here.

"You bet." The manager—at least she assumed he was a manager—who handed her the application looked about her age. That was encouraging. Or was it? Was getting on the managerial career track at Dealin' Dave's really the answer?

Stop, she told herself. You're just picking up an application. This isn't the rest of your life.

"Any questions?" The manager, whose nametag read "Travis," smiled at her. His face had the wind-burned, ruddy look of someone who spent a lot of time outside.

"What happens after I fill out the application?"

"You take a math test, and we look it over," he said. "If you meet our qualifications, we bring you in for an interview."

"A math test? You have to take a math test?" She couldn't remember the difference between a theorem and a postulate, and she'd barely squeaked through calculus in college.

"It's not bad. Basic addition, subtraction, multiplication, that sort of thing," said Travis. "I'm sure you'll do fine."

"Um, I got a 31 on my ACT!" said Renee brightly. "That's the 99th percentile!"

Travis smiled. "Uh huh. That's good to know. Well, you still have to take the math test. If you want to apply for a job here, anyway."

She nodded. "I see. My ACT score doesn't count for much, does it?"

"Far as I can tell, it doesn't count for anything."

"You are so right." She took the application. "Mind if I fill this out now?"

"Not at all. Come on." He led her back through the store, past the bathrooms, into a small kitchen with a long table and a scattering of chairs. "Enter the employee lounge." He handed her a pen. "I'm supposed to check that you don't have a calculator or laptop on you. Don't want you to cheat."

She showed him her hands. "Nothing, I swear. I'll pass or fail the math portion under my own power."

She filled out the front page of the application, pausing over the "current employer" section. Oh well. She put Mollie's name and the contact information for the mansion. She was going to have to find out Renee was leaving at some point.

The math test fortunately featured no questions about algebraic equations, lowest common denominators, or men getting on trains going in different directions at varying speeds. She had to add columns of figures, multiply sums, and figure out what 10 percent of $19.30 was. $1.93, right? You just moved the decimal point over. But maybe it was a trick question—one of those word problems that had a hidden clue that revealed the real, non-obvious answer. She read it three times, and then left the answer alone. If it was a trick, she couldn't figure it out.

The last page of the application was a short list of multiple-choice questions. Question 1 read: You're sitting on a bus, and the person sitting next to you gets up. As he does so, his wallet falls out of his pants. You: A. Get his attention and return his wallet. B. Look around to see if anyone else has seen the wallet fall out. C. Don't say anything but return if he realizes he dropped it. D. Slip it into your pocket. Renee stared at the page for a minute before circling "A." The rest of the questions were easy to answer — at least she thought so.

She walked back through the store, application in hand. The blond girl she'd seen here with Colleen saw her and noticed the application.

"Good luck!" she waved and gave her the thumbs-up. Renee waved back. Maybe she'd work here and some of Angel's perkiness would rub off on her.

Travis looked over the application as she stood there, her fingers laced together. "What's the 'C' for? Your application says 'C. Renee.'"

Renee made a face. "Candy. But I go by Renee?"

"Candy?"

"Please. No jokes. I've heard them all."

She was surprised when he nodded. "No problem." He underlined Renee on her application, then flipped to the math test.

"Did I do okay?"

He started marking it with a red pen, shaking his head. Then he looked up and saw her stricken face.

"I'm kidding!" He checked the application again. "You missed one. You pass."

"I missed one? Which one?" He showed it to her and she grimaced. "Oops."

"Sure about that ACT score?"

"Yeah, well, high school was a while ago."

"No worries. Besides, you didn't miss any of the HI questions. That's a bigger deal."

"HI questions?"

"Honesty Index." He showed her the page of multiple-choice questions. "It's a test that's supposed to indicate whether you'll defraud or steal from your employer."

"A one-page test can do that?"

"Between you and me, I doubt it. But the company likes the idea of having the tool." He shrugged, studying her application. "You live in St. Louis? What are you doing here?" He looked at her. "And why do you want to get out of the catering biz?"

"That is a long story," she said. "The short answer..." How to explain. Forget it. She'd aced the Honesty Index, so why start her new life with half-truths? "The mansion is my boyfriend's family business," she said. "Well, my former boyfriend's family business. We've been together for six years and we were going to get married — at least I thought so — and now we're not. And I work for his mom." Renee stopped herself. What was she doing? She must be nervous. This guy didn't want to know her life story, nor did she need to share it. She cleared her throat. "Can I just say it's complicated?"

"Sounds complicated." He glanced back down at the application, then at her. "But you still haven't answered my question of why here. Why suburban Chicago? Why Dave's?"

"I have family here. Well, practically family," she amended. "My best friend lives here."

Travis was still watching her. "Know anything about the store?"

"Not much," she admitted, then mentally kicked herself. "I know you're big on customer service, though, and having spent years working in the hospitality industry, I know how critical that is."

"You majored in art. How did you wind up in catering?"

She smiled. "I majored in art!"

He nodded. "I should have known. You're looking at a history/sociology double major here."

"Which naturally leads to a career in the retail food industry, right?"

"Anything else would be unthinkable!" Together they laughed off unfulfilled dreams, rude awakenings, years of expensive schooling, and even more years of yet-to-be paid college loans hanging over their heads. Travis reached over and shook her hand. "Give us a few days to look everything over. No promises, but I think you'll be getting a call for an official interview."

"What was this?"

"The first hoop."

"Sounds good. You can reach me on my cell or at that local number. Either one."

She waved as she left the store, hurrying to her car. She liked him. He appeared to be happy with his current position in life—that was rare. When she'd given up art—or at least the idea of doing it for a living—she'd taken it much harder. Maybe it had been unrealistic to think she could create art and make a living from it, but that didn't make accepting that she couldn't do it any less painful. She'd swung hard in the other direction. If art wasn't her career, she wouldn't bother with it at all. She'd dumped all of her card stock, her supplies, her books of paintings, and her mess of papers with note and calculations and contact names into five plastic bins and had shoved them into a closet. But she hadn't thrown them away. When she'd moved in with Lars, the boxes had been dragged along too, weighty evidence of her failure.

She started the car, pausing before she put it in reverse to back out of her parking spot. Where was that stuff now? She mentally searched the house, winding up at last in the basement. They were stacked in a neat pile in the corner, next to the washer and dryer.

She shouldn't have tried to make art her career. You were supposed to create art for yourself, to please your own sensibilities. A true artist never stopped to consider how an audience might react or how marketable her work was or how many pieces she had to sell to turn a profit. Those kinds of conventional monetary and business concerns had to be kept separate from the art itself lest they infect it. An artist must live for her art, be willing to risk everything, eschew friends and family who didn't understand her vision, survive on Ramen noodles and generous, better-heeled friends.

As an artist, you only had to please yourself. But to get people to buy your art, you had to please them as well. That was the catch-22. So she kept up her work as a wage slave, and tried not to think about whether she was truly an artist or had just played one in school. And once she had met Lars, making art hadn't seemed as important as it had before.

She drove to Colleen's, paying closer attention to the neighborhood. Mature trees, large yards, a mix of older homes and newer houses. She didn't see any apartment buildings, but one street had several duplexes.

The thought of looking for a new apartment depressed her. She pictured rundown buildings with industrial brown carpeting, strange cooking smells, old cigarette smoke, and doors that slammed shut in the middle of the night. She'd thought she was all done with apartment living when she'd moved into Lars' little bungalow near the mansion. It was the first time since Colleen had left for Chicago that she'd felt that she had a home. That she was home. She should have realized she was wrong.

Colleen thought she was joking at first. "What?"

"What would you think if I moved up here?"

"Are you serious?" Colleen turned from the counter, where she was peeling potatoes. "But what would you do?"

"Maybe work at Dealin' Dave's." Renee leaned up against the counter, watching for Colleen's reaction.

"Yeah, right."

Renee stepped closer to her, opening her arms. "No, I'm serious. Listen. What is there for me in St. Louis? I only moved there because you did, after all. Now my whole life there revolves around Lars. I work with his mom and sister all day long. I just can't see going back to work at the mansion and acting like it's no big deal!" She stopped and cleared her throat. "I can't do it, all right? I don't want to be his friend," she raised her fingers to make quote marks. "I don't want to keep him in my life and to act as if nothing has changed when it has."

"Are you sure? This is a huge decision." Colleen dumped the potatoes into a pan, and began peeling a large carrot. "You could go anywhere, you know."

Renee had thought Colleen would like the idea of her moving here. Of course, she'd been here for five days already. She was probably just overstaying her welcome. "I don't want to go anywhere else," said Renee. "I followed you to St. Louis. Can't I follow up you here?" She kept her tone light.

"Of course you can. You know that. I think that you should have some kind of plan, though. Not make a crazy decision out of…"

"Out of what?"

Colleen waved her hand. "Forget it. I'd love you to move here, really. I just want you to be happy."

"I know." Renee reached for a peeled carrot and took a bite. "Look. I've been thinking about this, and I don't want to go back to St. Louis. I don't want to start over there. Maybe Dealin' Dave's isn't the answer for the rest of my life, but I just need something now. I can certainly restock shelves and scan groceries and give balloons to kids. How hard can it be?"

She'd show up, punch a clock, unload boxes of wine for eight hours, and be done. The money might not be great, but she was used to living on a caterer's salary. Besides, she'd been setting aside money to pay for their wedding. It wasn't like she was broke. And at Dealin' Dave's, no one was going to call her at 10:30 at night with questions about the seating charts for a wedding reception that was still six weeks out, or decide to change the menu the day before a baby shower because it turned out the mom-to-be didn't care for mahi mahi.

"If you think it's the right thing…"

"I do. Hey, I may not even get the job! Wait until I get an offer, and then we can revisit the issue of whether I'm making a smart decision." Renee reached for another carrot. "Okay?" She didn't tell Colleen that she'd already made the decision not to return to St. Louis. Lars didn't want her—or he didn't want her enough. She wasn't going to go back and try to figure out how to make him an ancillary part of her life instead of the center. Besides him, the closest thing she had to a center was Colleen. If she was going to start over, why not start over here?

Chapter 6
Colleen

Colleen sat on the portable bleachers, her feet propped on the seat below her. Several other parents sat nearby, watching the pack of little boys in shorts and T-shirts charge after the basketball. Jordan's coach, Jamal, stood on the sidelines, his whistle in his mouth. He blew it, and the herd came to a halt, three boys fighting for the ball.

"Wait a minute. Houston, Ben, Raj, you're supposed to be playing a zone defense, remember? You're not supposed to gang up on Patrick."

Raj, the smallest but most ferocious player on the team, wiped his dark hark from his forehead. "But he's got the ball!"

Jamal put his hand on his shoulder. "Yes, I know. But this isn't football. You don't run after whoever has the ball and try to tackle them! Right?"

Most of the boys looked unconvinced, but Jordan stayed focused on Jamal. He stood with his lips pressed together, his hands on his hips. Even when a couple of the boys next to him whispered and shoved each other, he stood without moving, his face serious.

Jamal checked his watch and blew his whistle again. "That's it! Good practice. Remember the game is at 8:30 on Saturday morning. I'll see you then." Most of the boys dashed off the court where their parents were waiting, but Colleen saw Jordan lag behind to ask Jamal a question.

Jamal bent down to listen, thought for a moment, and then answered. Jordan nodded and walked slowly over, deep in thought. She offered him a bottle of water, and he took a long drink and caught her eye.

"Thank you." He rubbed his face. "That was a good practice!"

"It was," she agreed. "What were you asking Coach Jamal about?"

"How to make more shots."

"Really?" Jordan rarely got the ball, and then he didn't chuck into the air at the first opportunity like most of his teammates. "What did he say?"

"To practice more." He shoved his arm into his coat as she helped him shrug it on. "But how can I practice shooting when I hardly get the ball?"

Only four years old and already the world was turning out to be a difficult place. "You could practice other times."

He rolled his eyes in a perfect imitation of Taylor. "And when is *that* going to happen?"

"Jordan, watch your tone."

He bit his lip and looked down. "Sorry, Mommy. But I want to be the one who everyone throws the ball to."

Of course he did. Colleen smiled at her son, feeling that swirl of love and heartbreak. No one prepares you for this, that you'll live every disappointment, every letdown, every broken hope that your child has. And they never stopped coming.

"Why don't we talk to Daddy about it tonight? I bet if you ask him, he'd bring you here some nights after work to practice." She helped him into his puffy winter coat.

"But sometimes I'm already in bed when he gets home," Jordan pointed out. They climbed the stairs to the main floor together, Jordan stepping carefully so he didn't have to hold the handrail "like a baby."

"On other nights, then. Or on Sundays." She reached for his hand when they stepped outside and he didn't pull away the way he sometimes did.

"Sundays?" He looked up at her. He still hadn't mastered the days of the week.

"The day after your games." They reached the car, and she opened the door for him. He climbed up onto his booster seat and reached for the seatbelt.

"Mommy, I can do it myself!"

"All right." She watched him concentrate to snap the belt into place and smiled at him. "Perfect."

"Mommy? Don't let me forget to ask Daddy tonight, okay? Sometimes I forget."

She looked at him in the rearview mirror. His damp hair was sticking to his forehead, his face serious. "I won't let you forget," said Colleen.

"Promise?"

"I promise."

He nodded, satisfied. One more minor crisis averted, one more small victory in the ongoing battle that was parenthood. Now she'd just have to get Pete to do it — or bring him here herself.

She checked her watch. Five minutes 'til Taylor got out of school. Crap! She remembered Renee was home with the baby, and had offered to walk down to the school and pick her up. Colleen had agreed — after all, it was a sunny day, in the 40s, and the baby loved her stroller. She realized with a start that she didn't have to rush home to snatch up another kid. Right now she was blissfully responsible for just one.

"What do you say to some hot cocoa?" She looked at Jordan, who threw up his arms.

"I say YEAH!"

"All right." She turned left, heading toward Main Street.

"Mommy, can we go where we watch the trains?"

"I'm one step ahead of you, kiddo. That's where we're going."

"All right!" He threw up his arms again. "How many do you think we'll see?"

"I'm not sure. Want to make a bet?"

"Yeah. I'll say…seven."

"Seven? That's a lot. I'll say," she pretended to ponder the point. "I'll say seven hundred fifty-nine."

Jordan laughed. "Moo-ooom." He shook his head. "You know that's way too many. Come on. Bet real."

"All right then. I'll say…I'll say four." With any luck, seven trains would roll through in the next half hour or so, and Jordan would go home thrilled with winning his wager.

She parked and waited for Jordan to climb out before firmly shutting his door. The floor-to-ceiling windows on the north side of Caribou faced the train tracks, which made the coffee house one of Jordan's favorite places. Trains rolled east toward Chicago, 26 miles closer to Lake Michigan, and west toward Iowa. Commuter trains ran more frequently during rush hour, but the rest of the day freight trains hauling dozens of flatbeds rumbled through every few minutes. Jordan grabbed his hot chocolate and dashed toward a pair of chairs next to the window, climbing onto one backwards for a better view. "Are we starting counting now, Mommy?"

"Sure. Starting now!"

He craned his neck in both directions, and she sat down with her mocha. "Honey, take off your coat so you don't get overheated." He shrugged off his jacket without changing position. The warning bells started to ring, signal lights flashing, and he whipped his head back toward her. "Mommy! One's coming!"

"I know. See the gates going down?"

"Yeah. So the cars don't get hit."

"That's right. And why else?"

He pursed his lips without answering.

"So people don't cross in front of the train, right?"

"Right. That's stupid."

She nodded. People who tried to beat the train *were* stupid. And sometimes dead. Still, a little girl his age had been killed last year—running across the tracks to greet her daddy on the other side. The horror of that had never left her.

A trio of fortyish men, all in business suits, sauntered up to the counter, ordering a latte and two coffees. One glanced at her without interest. She was used to that. Eight years ago, she might have conducted a meeting with these guys. They might have asked her questions, sought her opinion about a new product launch, and maybe even engaged in a little harmless flirting. Now she was invisible.

Was it Jordan? Was it the way she was dressed? How had she become a complete nonentity to every man out there? It wasn't just the men—it was the women who worked, too. It seemed like everyone she met, even Pete's coworkers, asked polite meaningless little questions and made half-hearted friendly gestures when she encountered them. No one cared what she thought, or felt, or even whether she even had an opinion.

"Mommy! Look! Here comes number two!" Jordan pointed at an engine rumbling in from the west.

"That's right! Do you think it will be a passenger train or a freight train?"

He thought a moment. "Freight." He pointed at her. "You say passenger."

"Yes, sir!" She saluted and he laughed.

His face fell as the METRA commuter train went by. "It's passenger. You win." He slumped into his chair.

"Jordy, it's no big deal. Besides, we're counting the

trains, remember?"

He leapt back up, encouraged by the thought of winning again. All he needed was the possibility of winning to once again capture his attention. What did she need?

Renee had teased her about the stack of magazines piled next to the couch in the family room. *People. Us Weekly. The Star.* Even, she was ashamed to admit, *The Enquirer.*

"What are all these?" Renee had said, picking one up to look at it more closely. She started reading headlines aloud. "'Jen's secret heartbreak?' 'Jess and Nick's romantic getaway?' 'Who's gay in Hollywood?' You actually read this stuff?"

"So?"

"So, it's trash!" Renee flipped through a magazine at random. "Look at this! Some skinny drunk blond girl with her arm around another skinny blond girl."

"Paris Hilton. That's Lindsey Lohan on the right."

"Who?"

"Come on, you know who Paris Hilton is."

Renee thought. "Is she in that hamburger ad?"

"That's her."

Renee flipped through the magazines. "She's in all of these! Who is she?"

"Heiress to the Hilton fortune. Hollywood It girl of the moment."

Colleen could have told her much more. About Paris' feud with Nicole Richie. Her recent breakup with Paris Latsis, her former fiancé. About running off to Mexico with Stavros Niarchos, Mary-Kate Olsen's old boyfriend, and how it had broken Mary-Kate's fragile little heart. Colleen knew more than that, too. She knew Paris's eyes were really brown but she wore brilliant blue contact lenses. That her trademark stock-straight blond hair was naturally brown and curly. Colleen supposed that Paris would look like pretty much any 20-something in her natural state—sans hair dye, tinted contacts, and requisite designer wardrobe, anyway. "So? Col, why are you reading this stuff?"

Once again, Renee was talking down to her whether she realized it or not.

"It relaxes me, all right? If I want to curl up with a trashy magazine now and then, what's the big deal?"

Renee had dropped it. "Hey, forget it. It just doesn't seem like you."

Colleen hadn't bothered to try to explain to her. She couldn't read anymore—not books. She was too tired or too distracted or just too lazy to plow through a book anymore. But it took no effort to skim *People* or check out "stars with cellulite!" in the *Star*. And at the end of the day, she wanted something easy and brainless. What was wrong with that?

"Mommy!" Jordan grabbed her arm, nearly spilling her coffee. "Look! Another train! That's seven!" He held up his hands, splaying out all five fingers of one hand, and making a "peace" sign with the other. "Seven!" He looked at her for confirmation. "Right, Mommy?"

"That's right!" Colleen said, feeling a sudden rush of love for her little boy. "You win, kiddo." She hugged him. "You'll have to tell Taylor you beat me when we get home."

"Yeah!" He threw his hands up, and Colleen laughed. Most days she wanted her children to grow up, to be able to take care of themselves, to stop pestering her every minute, to stop needing her so much. But at moments like this her heart swelled, and she felt that soaring sense of love and amazement that she had been given—no, blessed with—her children, and she wanted to be nowhere else than exactly where she was. She gave a silent, quick prayer of gratitude for her life, and reached for her son's hand to head home.

As she turned toward their street, Colleen saw one of her neighbors outside and waved. Amelia waved back. She was one of the only women on their street who didn't have kids, but not for lack of trying, according to Melissa. Melissa was the street's "alpha mom," and had told Colleen that Amelia and her husband had tried in-vitro fertilization a "ton of times." Melissa had said that Amelia had told her she'd quit her job to focus on getting pregnant. So far it didn't appear to have helped.

She'd introduced herself to Amelia when she'd moved in, taking over a plate of brownies. Amelia had mentioned that she and her husband had just returned from a four-year stint in China. They'd lived in Europe for several years before that, and Colleen had been fascinated. Amelia was tall, with pale skin and clear blue eyes, and had a grace about her that Colleen envied. Colleen had been hoping that the two of them could become friends—she was fascinated by her life, so unlike her own.

Of course if Renee got the job at Dealin' Dave's and moved here, she'd have a real friend nearby. Too bad she still felt a distance between them. Yes, she and Renee had shared history, but she needed more than that. She wanted more than anything to be able to talk, really talk, to someone who would listen and not judge her. Yet while she was certainly friendly with some of the neighborhood moms, their play date conversations had never risen above the level of small talk and mom-to-mom commiseration. Yet the other women didn't seem to mind. Why did she?

Late the next morning, Renee returned from running errands, a smile on her face and a bag of groceries in her arms.

"Guess who the new Dave's employee is? I got it! I start on Tuesday!"

"No, no. That's hot." Colleen pulled the baby away from the oven. She was making cookies for Jordan's preschool class. Not homemade exactly—they were the refrigerated dough she preferred to eat raw — but she was baking the darn things. Taylor and now Jordan had expressed their need for school treats like everyone else's. That meant cookies on a plastic-wrapped plate, not out of a freshly opened package of Chips Ahoy. Although Colleen had seen some pretty suspiciously uniform cookies on paper plates, come to think of it.

"Yum! Cookie dough!" Renee picked up a dollop of dough and dropped it into her mouth. "So? What do think?"

"I think it's great. I do."

"Get this — they've offered me fulltime hours! And they're talking about possibly getting me on the management track."

"Already? You haven't even started."

Renee pulled off her long wool coat and hung it over the back of the chair. "I know. But it's kind of cool that they even suggested it."

"Have you said anything to Lars' mom?"

Renee had picked up the baby, who sat happily in her lap, reaching for her hair. Renee shifted her and pushed her hair behind her ear without looking down. "No," she admitted finally. "I was waiting until I got the job."

"So you're definitely doing it? You're definitely moving here?" She offered Renee a piece of cookie dough, popping one in her own mouth for good measure.

Renee ate it slowly. "Yes, I guess I am." Rose bounced up and down on her lap, and Renee let her stand on her lap, grabbing tightly onto her index fingers. "If I hadn't gotten the job, I suppose I might have gone back — but this feels like the right thing to do."

Colleen nodded. And waited.

"What do you think? Do you think it's the right thing to do?"

"What kind of honesty are you looking for?" The

reference went all the way back to their first year of college, when they had bonded over the shallow superficiality of so many of their classmates. Though in retrospect, they were probably just as shallow, Colleen realized now.

Of course *they* hadn't thought so, and so they'd developed their theory of honesty variations. First, there were flat-out, naked-faced lies—where honesty didn't even enter in. Things like, "officer, I had no idea I was driving that fast!" Then there was social honesty. This was the level you had with most people—where white lies were expected as a matter of course. No one wants to know what you really think of their new boyfriend, their haircut, or their clothing, after all, if you're going to be critical. They only want to hear the good stuff.

Then there was casual honesty, the kind that you used to show how completely cool and evolved and without hang-ups you were. Colleen knew other girls who had mastered this skill ("Oh, yeah, I lost my virginity when I was fourteen! That was before I started drinking and snorting coke and got kicked out of high school") but she'd never been able to shake the feeling that certain things just weren't for public viewing.

Finally, there was brutal honesty. Brutal honesty meant honesty without pretenses, intentions, or limitations. They'd sworn that's the kind they'd have with each other.

"But not all the time," Colleen had said. "We just have to know it's there. If we need it."

"Why not all the time?" Renee had asked.

"Think about it. That's too much pressure. What if you think my outfit makes me look like a skank or I don't like a guy you're dating or we get into some horrible argument about religion or something? We'd never be able to stick to it. We'd slide right back into social honesty to save the friendship."

"You're right. We'd start with little lies and it would escalate from there." Renee had reached over, her hand extended. "To brutal honesty. Or to know that we'll be brutally honest if we need it. I promise."

Colleen had shook Renee's strong, slightly callused hand. "Promise."

She looked at her friend now in the kitchen of her home. Renee's hair was longer and lighter now than she had worn it in college, when she dyed it jet black and cut it herself. Her skin was no longer dewy, and she had lines around her mouth and eyes. Her body was the same, though — small breasts and squarish torso, skinny arms and legs, strong, knobby fingers. She looked older but just as easily damaged as she had then. "Brutal?" said Colleen.

Renee put her hands out onto the table as if to steel herself. "I'm ready."

"I think..." Colleen started.

"Go on. Just say it. Brutal, right?"

"I think you're running away. I think you're angry and hurt, and instead of dealing with it, you're doing a 180 without thinking about the consequences. And Renee, why take a job already? You could travel. You could go anywhere. You don't have to put down roots here of all places."

"I know that." Renee laced her fingers together over the baby's belly, and Rose began tugging at them curiously. "I don't think I'm running away." She looked at Colleen. "All right, maybe I am. But 'running away' implies fear, doesn't it? I'm not afraid to go back. I don't *want* to go back. I'm choosing not to go back. See the difference?"

Colleen nodded and let it go. Renee may have asked for brutal honesty, but that didn't mean she wanted it.

Chapter 7
Renee

She'd looked at three apartments already, and was beyond discouraged. The first had been in a rundown building, the parking lot filled with rusted-out cars held together by little more than duct tape and hope. The second had been on the ground floor, and she hated the idea of people tramping about overhead all day long. The third had smelled strongly and unmistakably of cat pee.

Renee stopped at the Caribou by the train station on her way back to Colleen's, ordering a large nonfat latte. Some caffeine would set her straight.

She sat, sipping her coffee and watching the people in the shop. She had that odd sense of anonymity she'd been experiencing since she arrived two weeks ago. At home, she waved to the neighbors, greeted the college kids at the Starbucks by name. Even the checker at the grocery store smiled in recognition. St. Louis was a small town, after all, if not in size then in sensibility. There when someone asked where you went to school, they didn't mean college. They meant high school.

Here, she knew nobody but Colleen, Peter, and the kids. She could start from scratch. That's what she had wanted, right?

She should be delighted to look for an apartment, a

place of her own, a sign of her new life, her new independence. She could do anything, go anywhere, like Colleen had said. In college, she'd even flirted with the idea of moving to Alaska. She'd work on a fishing boat for a few crazed months and make enough to do her art fulltime in the off season. That hadn't happened—after all, it was easier to work in a bar at night than risk drowning, bodily injury, and reeking of fish guts for weeks on end. (And that was long before *Deadly Catch* had hit the airwaves, destroying any remaining romantic notions she may have had of that kind of life.)

Colleen didn't understand. Renee didn't want to travel or "go anywhere" she wanted. She wanted a home. Without the tether that had tied her to St. Louis for both work and love she felt as helpless as a party balloon in the breeze. She could accept that her life wouldn't be what she expected, but she couldn't go back and rebuild it with a big hole where Lars had been. She sighed. She missed him. She missed getting up in the morning and wrapping her body around him for a few minutes before she dragged herself out of bed. She missed his warmth, his smell, his grin.

But this had to be the right thing. She'd stay here, and make this place her new anchor. She needed something to tie her flighty self down. Better to pine away hundreds of miles away than to pine away under his nose, and hold out for the slim chance Lars would change his mind.

She might act like she was fine with Colleen, but she still couldn't quite believe this had happened. She had believed. She'd known from the moment he'd looked at her the first time they'd made love, down to the deepest part of her heart, that he was for her, and she was for him. She remembered the amazement she'd felt, the awe at being given a gift she didn't deserve and wasn't anticipating. That feeling, that belief, that truth had only grown with time. And try as she might, she couldn't just eviscerate everything she felt for him. There was still a stubborn little seedling sprouting in her heart that refused to die. That must be why she still hurt so much.

At least she'd had the courage to call Mollie, finally, after deciding an email was too impersonal. Before Renee had had a chance to launch into her explanation, Mollie had interrupted.

"Lars told me about you two, Renee," Mollie had said. "I am so very sorry."

Renee had nodded automatically, forgetting Mollie couldn't see her. "Thanks," she'd managed.

"And Lars told me you've found work up there?"

Renee started to apologize, but Mollie broke in again.

"Renee, you don't have to apologize to *me*. I can't say I'm happy, but I understand. I just wish I could shake some sense into that son of mine. He'll regret this, I know."

Renee had cleared her throat. "So, is everything at the mansion all right then?" That was easier, safer than asking about Lars.

"We're fine, honey, I swear. Don't worry about us. But don't be a stranger either! You know I consider you family."

Sure, Mollie did. But Lars didn't. Renee had managed to get off the phone without breaking down, or worse, crying on Mollie's shoulder. Your boyfriend's mother wasn't the appropriate place for sympathy, no matter how much she loved you.

Now she called the last place she'd circled on the classifieds from the coffee shop. A woman answered. She sounded as if she were having as bad a day as Renee.

"If you want to come now, fine," she said. "Otherwise we'll have to do it another day."

Renee agreed, asked for brief directions, and hurried out to the car. She pulled up to the house—a Victorian pink and white three-storied monster with a wraparound porch. A three-car detached garage sat behind the house, with an outdoor staircase that led to a second story apartment.

It wasn't her imagination. The woman showing her the place was definitely unhappy. Renee guessed she was in her late 40s, with a broad, flat face, wide shoulders, and narrow hips. She was wearing a charcoal pantsuit that made her look broader than she was, and her eyes looked tired and pouchy.

The apartment had the musty, empty smell of unoccupied space but that was worlds better than the cat-pee place. The layout was simple; the door opened onto a small living area, with a kitchen off to the left, a full bathroom to the right. The bedroom was at the back of the apartment, facing south. Like the living room, it had large windows that made up for the relative lack of square footage. Renee imagined looking out the window when the huge maple trees were in leaf. It would be like nestling into her own little tree house. The kitchen had a built-in breakfast bar under another big window, with stained glass diamonds of red, blue, and gold on either side.

It was unique. It was different. It was her. Renee cleared her throat. "How much is it?"

"$700 a month, including heat and water."

"And I can park in the driveway?"

"Long as you stay to the right."

Renee looked around. She'd need to buy more furniture—a bed came to mind—but that wasn't a problem. It was cute, cheap, and close to Dealin' Dave's. And it felt personal, not nondescript like those horrible apartments she'd already seen.

She signed a one-year lease without bothering to read it closely. Vicki—that was the woman's name—had warmed up to her as soon as she'd agreed to take the place, but Renee didn't expect to find any home-baked cookies waiting for her when she moved in.

Who cares, thought Renee. She had a place to live, and could stop camping out at Colleen's. She'd been so discouraged about finding an apartment, and look what had happened! She was starting her new job tomorrow. Maybe this was the beginning of only good things.

The next morning, Renee was up early. She made coffee and sat reading *The Trib*, listening to the sounds of Colleen's house waking up. She heard Taylor's high-pitched voice, followed by Colleen's lower one. Then Jordan came clomping down the stairs, still in his pajamas, followed by Colleen, carrying Rose on her hip. She wore her ubiquitous chinos and a long-sleeved tan and black striped shirt. You'd never guess she had three kids, thought Renee. She still looked like the 18-year-old she'd met in college.

"Want a hand?" She watched as Colleen poured cereal into the older kids' bowls, balancing the baby.

"I've got it." Colleen poured herself a cup of coffee and topped off Renee's. "Nervous?"

"Yeah, I am. How stupid is that?"

"It's a new job. Of course you're going to be nervous."

"I'm going to be stacking cans, Col. I think I can handle it."

The truth was, Renee was looking forward to something as uncomplicated and foolproof as stacking cans or unloading boxes. How hard could it be? Arrange the cans so the labels were all facing the right direction. Restock merchandise. Bag groceries. The idea of doing these simple, physical tasks was undeniably appealing. How much brainpower did bagging groceries take? Be careful not to overload the bag or to put bananas or bread on the bottom and you were more than halfway home.

Still, she *was* nervous. She arrived at the store a few minutes early. She was wearing new jeans and a red pullover fleece under her winter coat. She looked casual but not sloppy — at least that's what she hoped. She looked around for Travis, but he wasn't there.

"Um, good morning. I'm Renee Leighton? Today is my first day?"

The woman at the manager's desk had at least six inches on her. She looked up from the computer, with a slight frown. "I'm sorry? How can I help you?"

Geez, did she not get the memo about friendliness? "Renee Leighton. I'm new? This is my first day?"

Pam, the woman's nametag read. Renee waited.

"Oh, a new hire. Hang on a minute." Pam turned her attention back to the screen, frowning again. Renee looked around the store. It wasn't busy yet; there were just a few shoppers wandering the aisles. A couple of employees were joking with each other as one arranged packages of cookies next to a register. Renee smiled at them, feeling stupid.

"Did you get a vest yet?"

"Um...no. It's my first day?" Renee hated how wimpy she sounded, but she wanted to err on the side of polite. She shifted her weight to her other hip, fighting a sudden urge to curl a piece of hair around her finger.

Pam looked up, finally, as if seeing her for the first time. She frowned for a moment. "I didn't interview you."

"Um, no." Renee stood there for a moment. "Travis did. Want to interview me now?" she said brightly, with no trace of sarcasm. Pam looked at her more closely — a calculating look. She was about Renee's age, with smooth olive skin and dark red hair. Her eyes were a striking green, and contrasted with her skin tone, giving her an exotic, almost cat-like look. She had the kind of beauty that men noticed and women envied, and Renee immediately felt scrawny and boyish in comparison.

Before Pam could respond, a customer approached, a Dealin' Dave's bag in her hand. "Excuse me." She held a bag of mixed greens in her hand. "I bought this yesterday and it's not fresh."

Pam reached for the lettuce and nodded her head. "I am so sorry about that. We'll be happy to replace it. Or we can refund your money."

"Yes, I'd like to replace it."

"Shall I have someone go get a new bag for you?"

"No, that won't be necessary." The woman folded her Dealin' Dave's bag under her arm. "I have more shopping to do, so I'll get it myself."

"All right. Again, I'm truly sorry that that happened. Let the person who checks you out know that you've got a credit for another bag."

The woman waved her off, displaying a large diamond on her left hand. "I will. And thank you."

Renee had watched the exchange, noting how graciously Pam had handled it. She hadn't questioned the customer or argued with her; she'd given her several options to choose from, which let her feel in charge; and most important of all, she'd apologized. And she'd meant it.

Renee knew when a guest was unhappy, the first thing you did was apologize—as sincerely as you could. Then you made it right. "That was nicely handled," she said.

Pam looked back at her. "Oh. Yes. We guarantee all of our products."

Renee nodded. "Yes, that's one of the things that interested me in the store. The commitment to customer service."

Pam looked at her sharply again. Renee suspected she wasn't sure whether Renee was being completely sincere.

"Yes. We're about happy customers. A happy customer is a loyal customer."

Renee nodded and smiled. Hopefully she'd win her over with her attention to customer service.

Pam stepped out from behind the manager's counter. "Let me take you back and get you set up."

She followed Pam to the back of the store, noting how she smiled and greeted every customer they came near. Well, she could certainly do that as well.

"Here you go." Pam handed over an enormous brown binder that was cracked down the seam. "We'll have you read the first five sections of the Dealin' Dave's manual. When you finish, come up to the front."

She left the room, the door swinging shut behind her, and Renee slowly sat down, pulling the manual closer so she could read it. It was faster going than she thought. She read up on proper lifting (always use your legs, not your back) and box-cutting techniques (hold the box-cutter in your dominant hand and cut away from your body, never toward it) along with the importance of good grooming and attentive customer service.

"A customer should never have to locate an associate to ask a question or find an item," the manual said. "An associate should always be nearby, ready with a friendly greeting or offer of assistance."

That sounded like it could be challenging in practice, thought Renee. Were employees, or rather associates, supposed to play some kind of man-to-man defense on the customers? She already knew she wouldn't bring that question up to Pam.

When she finished the manual, she tucked it back on the shelf Pam had retrieved it from, and worked her way back up through the store. "I'm finished," she said brightly.

"You read the first five sections already?" Pam's voice and tone said that she doubted that could be true.

"I'm a fast reader," apologized Renee.

Pam looked over her shoulder. "Angel! Angel, could you step over for a moment?"

Renee recognized her from her earlier trips to the

store and smiled. "Hi there."

"Hey! How's your day treating you?"

"Angel, this is…" Pam looked at Renee expectantly.

"Renee," Renee supplied.

"Renee. She's a new hire. You're on the floor right now. Would you show her the fresh and produce sections?"

"Sure thing." She beckoned, and Renee stepped quickly behind her. "Did Pam get you a vest?"

Renee shook her head. "Huh uh."

"Come on, we'll do that first. There are a couple of cute ones back there." She looked at Renee. "You need a medium, right? No, probably a small."

In a closet in the back of the employee room, Angel dug out and pulled out a handful of brightly colored patterned vests. "What do you think?"

"Oooh." Renee reached for the lime green and bright pink pattern, discovering it was made up of pink flamingos and palm leaves. "I love this one."

"I've got that one too!" Angel grinned. "Pick one more."

Renee chose another equally vivid vest and followed Angel out to the store.

"Okey doke. This," Angel gestured, indicating a refrigerated section that ran along most of the length of one wall, "is 'fresh.' It includes the cold produce, sushi, pre-made sandwiches, yogurt, and milk." She walked along the aisle, pointing out various items. "Everything fresh has a sell-by date on it." She held up a package of California rolls. "See the orange sticker on here? 02/02? That's it."

Renee nodded.

"So, when you do fresh, you front and face everything. You know what that means, right? You bring all the product up to the front, and make sure it's facing the right direction."

Renee nodded. "Makes sense."

Angel bent to replace the package of sushi, straightening the other packages as she did so.

"Excuse me." Renee felt a hand gently touch her sleeve. "I'm looking for the meatless meatballs?"

"Ummm..." Renee looked desperately to Angel.

"Meatless meatballs! No problem!" Angel strode toward the center of the store, waving the elderly woman along. "We'll get you fixed up." Renee trailed behind, slowing her pace to walk next to the woman.

"Sorry," she said to the woman. "It's my first day."

"Your first day? How nice." The woman's head bobbed slightly as she walked. "My granddaughter brought me to this store. It's her favorite. She's a vegetarian, you know."

Renee nodded. "How old is your granddaughter?"

"She's twenty now. She's a junior at the University of Chicago. She is very bright," the woman said with no trace of pride. She was just stating a fact.

"I'm sure she is."

They'd reached the frozen food section, and Angel bent to pull out a bag of meatballs, exposing an intricate tattoo on her lower back as she did so. The initial "A" was surrounded by multicolored swirls of ink.

"How many bags would you like?"

"Just one, dear." The woman reached for the bag and set it down carefully in her shopping cart. "Thank you so much. Thank you too, dear," she said, addressing Renee. "And good luck with your first day."

Renee and Angel watched her toddle slowly away. "What a nice lady."

Angel nodded, pulling her shirt back down over her hips. Renee gestured at her waist.

"That's an amazing tattoo."

"Oh, that." Angel waved it off. "I've got six of them. That one's kind of boring."

"Six? Where are they all?" Renee immediately regretted the question, but Angel began ticking them off on her fingers.

"A daisy on my ankle. That was my first. Barbed wire on my both arms. An angel on my right shoulder—get it?" She stopped for a moment. "Oh! And a ladybug on my butt. That's it."

"Don't they hurt?"

Angel shrugged. "Depends on where you get them. The first tat—the one on my ankle—that killed. But the other ones weren't as bad. It's something to do with how much fat or muscle or something the needle's going into."

Renee nodded. She was the only person at the mansion without any ink. Even Mollie—who was older than her own mom—had a little butterfly on her shoulder. Renee was intrigued with the idea of using your body as a canvas, but a tattoo's permanence scared her. Besides, the majority of tattoos were only copies of someone else's idea—barbed wire, or Chinese symbols, animals, cartoon characters. Rarely did she see a tattoo that was truly different. If she was going to express herself through her skin, it would have to be something completely original—something she wanted to make part of her forever.

"If you want to see some amazing ink, have Dylan show you his back. He's got this radical Chinese dragon with all the symbols of the Chinese zodiac around it. He's got like 200 hours into it and he's not even finished." Angel shook her head in reverence. "It's off the hook."

"I'll have to check that out," said Renee, intrigued. She followed Angel back to the fresh section, where she showed Renee the colorful hand-written signs that accompanied each item. "Who makes those?" asked Renee.

"The tags? Oh, we have a girl who comes in every month or so. She does the signs, too," Angel gestured at the chalkboard signs overhead. "She gets paid to sit and draw, basically. Now that's a job."

Angel left Renee pulling codes, or removing the products in fresh that were past the sell-by date. It was slow going, looking at each individual cup of salsa, package of hummus, and sandwich wrap and carefully restacking them. After an hour, Renee's back ached from leaning forward and reaching to the back of the case. She was finishing the fresh soups section when Angel appeared at her side.

"I'm on the register, and you're supposed to shadow me."

"I'm going to learn how to work the register already?"

"Come on, it's no biggie. It'll take you five minutes."

Renee followed her up to the front of the store. Angel showed her how to enter her employee number to unlock the register, and how to slide items so the UPC triggered the infrared scanner. If it didn't scan, you slid it again until a beep sounded and the price appeared on the screen. "Some stuff will come up 'item not found,'" said Angel, as she scanned a cart full of groceries for a woman with a curly-haired toddler in the seat of her cart. "Then you punch in the UPC by hand." She showed her.

"Cash, that's easy. Ring it in as cash. Hit check for checks and credit for credit or debit cards, and then the customer runs the card through that little machine." Angel pointed at it, resting her weight on one foot, her head cocked to one side. She waited a minute, then asked the woman to sign the machine. "Oops! No, you have to use that stylus thingie, not a pen."

Transaction complete, she thanked the woman and began bagging her groceries. Her movements were remarkably swift. In a few moments, she had deposited three paper bags of groceries into the back of the cart. "Have a super day!" she said, then turned back to Renee with a swish of her ponytail. "See? No biggie."

But what if an item won't scan? What if I give the wrong change? What if it takes me too long to bag stuff? Renee's worries must have shown on her face because Angel laughed. "Just ring this bell twice if you need help, and someone will help you. You'll be fine."

Chapter 8
Colleen

Date night. When Taylor was born, she and Peter had dutifully agreed that once a week they would have an official night all to themselves. A night to spend reconnecting, talking about things more meaningful than which of the cars needed an oil change or whether Jordan's adorable little lisp amounted to mere baby charm or required expert intervention or where they would go for vacation this summer. It had started out as a weekly date, then slid to semi-weekly, and now was supposed to be a monthly occurrence. Hey, at least they were trying.

Colleen changed out of the T-shirt and pulled on an eggplant-covered wrap dress, one of her favorites. She rearranged her breasts and adjusted her cleavage, turning to check her reflection. In her grownup clothes, she had to admit she looked pretty good. Sure, she was a little thicker around the waist than she had been, but her shape hadn't changed that much over the years. Of course that's what happened when you sprout C-cup boobs and childbearing hips at thirteen years of age.

"Curves," her mom had said. "You have beautiful curves." And Colleen had believed her. She'd never understood why so many girls in high school and college starved themselves or bemoaned imaginary patches of cellulite. Then once she'd had kids, she'd encountered grown women doing the same thing—starving themselves to look like teenagers again, when they hadn't even liked the way they looked then. It was only when she compared herself to other women that she felt dissatisfied with hers—too large, too busty, too much. Then she'd gotten hooked on watching *Biggest Loser* and her body image had immediately improved. Compare yourself to someone worse off and you always felt better.

Colleen walked downstairs to find Renee sitting on the floor with Taylor and Jordan, dealing cards. "I'm teaching them crazy eights," she said. The baby sat between her legs, gnawing on a stuffed rabbit. "Peter said he's warming up the car."

Colleen smiled. Her husband had definitely gotten smarter over the years. A few months after Taylor was born, he'd made the mistake of having to gas up and stop for cash on one of their date nights. She'd sat with her arms crossed across her chest, her breasts already starting to fill, and had felt ridiculously angry. She'd exploded when he'd climbed back in the car.

"This is supposed to be a *date*! The car should be ready!" Then she had started sobbing, and had insisted on going home, startling the babysitter who was lying on the couch watching TV. She'd told the sitter it was an upset stomach. To Peter, she'd blamed hormones. They'd laughed about it eventually, though, and now he said he's learned his lesson. Date night, he had his car gassed up and ready to go, with cash in his wallet.

Colleen stood watching her children. Taylor was sitting close to Renee, their thighs nearly touching, and Jordan had his tongue sticking out as he tried to hold his cards in one hand. Renee noticed and reached for the cards, arranging them in a small fan for his hand to grasp. The baby slapped at Renee's thighs, gurgling happily. It was the picture of domestic bliss. Her kids didn't ignore

Renee, squabble with her, or roll their eyes when she asked them to do something. Even Taylor had been insisting on wearing her hair in a long low ponytail like Renee's.

"Ready to go?" Renee asked. "You look great. Hey, kids, doesn't your mommy look pretty?"

The older kids nodded without interest, and Renee and Colleen shared a smile. Sitting with the kids, Renee could almost pass for their high school babysitter. Not Colleen. Motherhood had aged her. She'd heard other women joking about the wrinkles or gray hair or extra ten pounds that kids bestowed, and Colleen joined in. But it went so much deeper than that. Her life had been divided into two parts: before kids and after. She could barely remember the before part.

Except I slept, she thought. And I didn't worry all the time. And...and what? And I was in love with my husband.

Pete appeared at the back door. "Your chariot awaits, my lady."

"Be right there." She briefly kissed the kids good-bye, who barely acknowledged her departure. "We won't be late."

Renee waved her off. "Stay as long as you want. Come on, you've got a free sitter!"

She was quiet on the drive to the Mediterranean restaurant they both liked, and Peter looked over at her. "Thinking of conversation topics?" That was part of the date itself—that they talk about things that did not involve cars, children, finances, home repairs, or errands.

She smiled briefly. "No. Just sort of blank."

"Want to tell me about your week?" They were pulling into the parking lot, and he got out first to open the door for her.

"Why don't you tell me about yours?"

They were seated, and the college-aged waitress stopped by immediately. She ordered a glass of merlot and

Peter, a Sam Adams. She smiled. Forget how expensive or high-class a restaurant was. He'd eschew the wine list for a Sam Adams or a Heineken, with not a thought to how it would look. He didn't like the taste of wine, and didn't drink hard liquor.

She watched him as the waitress served their drinks. "Would you give us a few minutes? Let us have a chance to look over the menu."

"No problem." Their waitress, a petite, pretty girl with dark hair, smiled at both of them and strolled away from the table.

"What?" He glanced at her. "We want more time, right?"

She took a sip of her wine. Smoky, rich, almost overpowering. She swallowed and sighed. "No, that's not it." She drank more wine. "I still love you."

He smiled and reached for her hand across the table. "That's fortunate. Because I *still*," he emphasized the word as she had, "love you, too."

She gripped his fingers more tightly. "No, that's not what I mean. I mean I truly love you. In a way I can't even explain to you."

He looked at her face closely, eyebrows lifted. "Want to try?"

She took another swallow of wine. "Remember when we first fell in love? And then when we lived in that tiny apartment off of Fullerton? And that weekend we stayed in bed the entire time?" She looked away from him. "I miss that."

He squeezed her fingers. "I miss it, too. But look what we have now. We've got three great kids, a nice house, we're not scraping by paycheck to paycheck anymore...look how far we've come since then."

"I know that." He wasn't getting it, she could tell. "I know how lucky we are. I just mean that I miss when it was just you and me."

"We were young and stupid," he pointed out. "And broke."

"I know we were young and stupid and broke. Maybe I miss being young and stupid and broke. Maybe not broke," she amended. "But young and stupid—why not?"

He pulled his fingers away and took a drink of his beer. "Want to give me a road map of this conversation? It started with declarations of love and now seems to be spiraling down into depressive self-reflection. Are you sure this is date conversation?" he said in an attempt to lighten the mood.

She got the message and dropped it. "Sorry." She didn't think he would understand anyway. They had everything. Who was she to complain? Look at the families who had lost their homes, everything they owned, their pets, even children to Hurricane Katrina. Or the tsunami that had killed thousands. And she was whining that she missed the time when all that mattered was curling up with him at the end of the day to watch *Seinfeld*. Could she be anymore selfish?

Maybe she hadn't phrased it right. She'd been trying to give him an incredible compliment, not wallow in regret. She'd meant what she'd said. She loved him more in some ways. But it was harder to love him, too. The feeling was still there, but it was buried under her fatigue and battling with Taylor and shoring up Jordan's fragile sports-related self-esteem and wiping up yet another pile of baby spit-up and running the kids to school and to the Y and to the doctor and to the library and then just running the house which meant trips to the dry cleaner and the bank and to Blockbuster to drop off the movies that she hadn't even managed to watch and the interminable trips to the grocery store where she always managed to forget something—formula or bread or toilet paper or something else of significance...she caught herself. This was date night. This was their opportunity to connect, and just as important, escape from the kids for a few hours. The waitress returned and Colleen ordered another glass of wine. She'd quench that small surge of panic swimming in her. He didn't deserve to be her personal dumping ground.

They ordered their dinner, and conversation wandered into the kids, as it always did. That was the charade of date night. No matter what they said, no matter how many promises they made ahead of time, they would wind up talking about the kids.

She could feel a slow irritation starting to bubble inside, the result of nearly three glasses of wine. She pushed the glass away and drained her water. She could feel she was on the bubble. Any more to drink and she'd plummet over the edge of self-control. She'd get nasty, pick at him for stupid things that most of the time didn't bother her. She might accuse him of forcing her to quit her job when she knew that wasn't the case. She might cry and suggest that they sell their house and move back to the city. She might start to seduce him, then lose interest before she finished. All of these outcomes were possible. The only constant would be her unhappiness and dissatisfaction, and his inability to understand why the woman he loved was so enraged or bitter or desolate or exhausted.

She wished she could chalk it up to sleep deprivation, but it wasn't just fatigue. That might explain some of her short-temperedness. But sometimes her anger scared her, the way it exploded into life from nowhere. Stupid things, little things—running to grab the phone only to discover it was a phone solicitor, forgetting the baby's cereal at the store, discovering Taylor had forgotten her backpack at school yet again—triggered a splattering rage, even as her rational self stood over her shoulder and said, "what are you getting so worked up about?"

She managed to keep it in check most of the time, dribbling out muttered expletives so the kids wouldn't hear. Surely this was the first step on the road to bag-lady-dom, mumbling her personal litany of how the world was failing her. A shabby coat, a few overloaded bags bulging with tattered blankets, and a crazed look in her eye, and she was there. Except for the kids, of course. She'd never seen a bag lady with kids in tow. The thought cheered her.

Surely this anger couldn't be good for her. She'd read countless times that stress could cause disease, and that only made her feel worse. She had a stable (if not always engaged) relationship, happy (most of the time) thriving kids, and enough money to drop $70 on a blouse without sacrificing something for it. She had the luxury of unlimited time with her children, and no longer had to endure the commute into the city, unpaid overtime, and the creeping realization that while her job paid well, it wasn't what she wanted to do with the rest of her life. As a stay-at-home mom she didn't have to deal with any of that, or even with the question of what she would do next. The years ahead of her had already been mapped out, like it or not.

Colleen excused herself and went to the bathroom, washing her hands with care. Pete deserved better. There was no reason for her to be angry, or ungrateful, or even annoyed. She needed to try harder, to stop the slide into self-pity and unmitigated self-reflection. She came back from the bathroom, drained a big glass of water, and put on her happy wife face. And it worked. This time.

Several days later, Colleen drove the short distance to Renee's new apartment. Jordan and the baby were strapped in the backseat, him in his booster seat, the baby in the infant seat that had survived three rounds of puke and diaper blowouts. Rose didn't seem to care, though, and kicked her feet, blowing spit bubbles.

"Are there going to be toys at this store?" asked

Jordan.

"Maybe a few, but it's more a store for grownups."

Jordan scowled. "Everything is for grown-ups."

Yeah, right. "That's not what it looks like from my perspective, kiddo," said Colleen, waiting at a four-way stop for another car.

"What's 'spective?'"

"Perspective. It's a way of looking at something." She looked at his face in the rearview mirror. "Like if you were lying on the ground, things would look different to you than if you were standing up. Because you'd have a different perspective."

"If I was lying down, like in the grass?"

"Right."

"If I was lying down in the grass, I'd see bugs. I'd see ants. And I'd smash them."

"But what about when you were standing up?" she said, ignoring his insecticide fantasies. She waited. "Would you still see ants?"

"Maybe..." he made eye contact with her in the mirror. "But they'd look smaller."

"Exactly!" She hit the steering wheel with her hand. "Because you've got a different perspective, see?"

He pulled the string from his sweatshirt back into his mouth. "Uh huh."

"So you learned a new word today, huh?"

"Yeah."

"Why don't you tell your daddy when he gets home. Or ask Taylor if she knows what it means."

"Oooh!" He kicked his feet gleefully. "I bet she won't know *this* word!" The baby caught his excitement, and began kicking harder, crowing. Jordan was forever competing with his older sister in sports, smarts, and of course, who was the favorite. She'd thought sibling rivalry wouldn't be an issue because they weren't the same gender. That had turned out to be yet another misconception of parenting.

"Huh, mommy? Huh? I don't think Taylor will know per-, per-,"

"Perspective," she supplied.

"She won't know it, right? And I will!" He threw back his head and crowed.

There was nothing more satisfying to a four-year-old than his taller, stronger, smarter sister being one-upped. Colleen smiled at him in the mirror. She would never admit she had a favorite, but she couldn't deny that Jordan was an easier child to love than Taylor. Jordan didn't fight her on everything, and he still snuck in their room early in the morning to cuddle. Maybe it would have been easier with all boys. Lots of dead bugs, muddy tennis shoes, and wrestling fights but none of the pushback not the mention the female friendship angst she was negotiating with Taylor now.

"Can we see Renee's house?" Jordan asked, reaching to unbuckle his seatbelt.

"No. Not today. We need to help Renee find furniture, remember? We'll see her house after the furniture is all done."

He slumped back in his seat, fingers still on the buckle. "All right."

She was surprised and relieved at his compliance. "Here comes Renee now! Maybe she'll want you to help her pick out her new furniture! Do you think you could do that?"

Renee climbed into the car, giving Colleen a brief hug. "Thanks for driving. Hi, kiddos!"

"Hi."

"That's a nice sweatshirt. What team is it?"

"The Bears!" Jordan arched his back to throw his chest forward. "Chicago Bears!"

"You think about what you need?"

Renee buckled her seat back and sighed, pushing

her hair out of her eyes. "I've got a couple of chairs, but I was thinking like a small couch or a loveseat. And I need a bed. Maybe a futon. I don't know." She turned to Colleen. "I figure you'll steer me in the right direction."

"And me! I'm going to help!"

"Oh, good." Renee turned so she could see Jordan. "I need a male perspective."

Colleen laughed and caught Jordan's eye. It took him a second. "Hey! I know that word!"

"You know perspective?" Renee widened her eyes. "Wow. That's a pretty big word."

"Well, I'm a big boy. I'm not a little boy anymore."

"You don't have to tell me that! I remember when you were a tiny baby. Smaller even than Rose."

"You do?"

"I do. You cried all the time. Waaaah waaaah waaaah. The only time you didn't cry was when your mom held you."

Jordan looked to her for confirmation and Colleen met her son's eyes in the mirror. "You didn't cry all the time," she said. "But you did cry sometimes."

"But I don't remember it!"

"That's because you were a baby. Not a big boy like you are now." It worked. Satisfied, he sucked on the sweatshirt string, looking out the window.

"How about lunch after?" Renee glanced at her. "I didn't realize you'd bring the kids—I was thinking of that Italian place on Ogden."

"What'd you think I was going to do with them? Leave them at home?"

Renee didn't seem to notice her tone. "No, of course not. I just thought you'd have a sitter since we were going shopping."

"Renee, I don't just have a sitter on standby. *I'm* the sitter, remember?"

Renee put her hands up. "Hey, it's no big deal. I just

thought it would be more fun if we were sans kiddies, that's all."

And it would be. They wouldn't have to sit in a noisy family-friendly restaurant with high chairs and easily wiped surfaces, and Colleen wouldn't have to snatch at her lunch in quick, unsatisfying bites while entertaining Jordan and making sure the baby didn't turn her cracker into a missile. But that meant planning ahead, and Renee hadn't given her the heads-up. One more example of how she had no idea of what Colleen's life was like anymore.

Chapter 9
Renee

When she got home that night, she turned on the overhead light, hanging her coat behind the door. The apartment that had looked so welcoming and cozy in the sunlight now appeared dreary and depressing. Renee mentally shook herself and took a quick shower, letting the hot water beat on her neck and right shoulder. She would have never imagined how sore she'd be after hours of scanning groceries. It was simple enough, but using the same muscles over and over left her feeling hunched like Quasimodo.

In the kitchen, Renee put water on for tea, rotating her neck back and forth. The apartment was silent except for the faint popping of the gas burner and the eventual hiss of the kettle. Renee sat at a stool at the built-in table, tracing the cracked surface with her finger. She missed the noise and light and energy of Colleen's house, Taylor sidling up next to her on the couch, Jordan pestering her to play crazy eights. And she missed the dense warm weight of Rose.

Sure, Colleen had said that she could stay as long as she wanted, but Renee had started to feel she was overstaying her welcome after just a few days. At first it had felt so good, so comfortable, to be there. But Colleen wasn't the same person. She'd recessed, pulled inward somehow. Before Renee had known that she could say something to Colleen and Col would get it, no explanations necessary. That to Renee was the measure of true friendship—getting each other.

No doubt Colleen was more important to her than the other way around. Maybe if she had a sister, or even a brother, she wouldn't feel so adrift. But growing up as an only child, she had always hoped for a sister—especially a big sister, someone who would always look out for her. She'd had few friends growing up, no one special. Her closest friend in high school was a sweet, talented boy, all elbows and gawky knees. People had thought they were dating, but they never even kissed.

Renee thought they'd both been afraid, not of ruining the friendship, but of their own as-of-yet-unexplored sexuality. She and Martin had smoked cigarettes and listened to the Cure and bemoaned the angst-ness of the artistic existence together. Unlike Renee, he had always known that he would succeed as an artist. He'd dropped out their senior year to go to New York to attend art school. He'd written a couple of times, and then they'd emailed sporadically. The last time she'd heard from him, he'd been making small, intricate sculptures out of paper clips, staples, and post-its. "Office Art" he'd called them, and apparently he'd found a gallery to give him a show. He'd done it—made it as an artist. And she...she was bagging groceries.

Renee got up to pour more water into her cup. This was better than the alternative. It had to be. She couldn't have started over living in St. Louis. She'd taken control. She hadn't let herself be the victim of circumstance, and that was something. She'd found a job. She'd found a place to live. She'd even borrowed Colleen's minivan and driven back to St. Louis to collect her possessions—not that she had that much. Almost all of "their" furniture was actually

Lars', and she wound up taking little more than a pair of mission-style chairs she'd bought on Craigslist, her battered bookshelf full of art books, and a couple of end tables she'd decorated with mosaic tiles as a post-college project. The furniture, her clothes, a few boxes of candles, dishes, towels, and toiletries, and her art supplies barely filled Colleen's car. She'd left Lars a note, relieved that she hadn't had to see him. She wasn't ready for that.

Renee got up and lit some candles. This place wasn't that bad. The light in the morning through the stained glass windows was beautiful, and she liked the lean, spare furniture she'd chosen from Ikea. She'd even splurged on a cranberry-colored couch with an undulating back, and Colleen had helped her choose a throw rug with a pattern of circles and lines.

"This place is perfect, Renee. It's a perfect little hideaway," Colleen had said, when she'd first seen it. Renee had been surprised. She'd been bracing herself for Colleen to say that the apartment was too small or that she was paying too much, or that she should have chosen to buy and not waste her money on rent. But Colleen had walked through the place, opened some cabinets, looked out the window at the still-bare trees, and sighed. "It's just the right place for one person." Then she had grabbed Rose, who had crawled into the bathroom and was busily pulling shampoo and lotion bottles out of the cabinet. "Like I said, one person." She'd left with Rose a few minutes later.

The next morning, Renee was out of bed at 5:20, which gave her time to shower, dress, and make it to the store by 6 a.m. She made coffee, pouring it into her travel mug. It was her fifth day in a row, and she was dragging. It wasn't the hours, but the way they'd been scheduled. She'd opened one day, worked a regular day shift the next two, and then worked the closing shift last night. Pam didn't seem to consider the fact that closing the night before you opened didn't leave a lot of time for other activities, including sleep.

At the store, she pulled the sliding glass store doors open by hand, shutting them behind her. She hung her coat in the back and punched in, noting the blare of the *Red Hot Chili Peppers* from the store's speakers. Renee smiled. That meant Pam wasn't here.

Sure enough, Travis waved at her from where he was mopping by the fresh section.

"Morning! You bring coffee for everyone?"

"Um, no." Renee stopped. "I didn't even think of it."

He laughed, and shook his head. "What kind of team player are you?"

"A tired one," she said, clipping her box cutter on her jeans and taking a drink of coffee. "I closed last night."

"What are you doing here today then?"

"That's a question I wouldn't mind having answered myself," she said, rearranging some bananas so they were no longer in danger of toppling onto the floor. "But that's what the schedule said."

"Ah, yes, the schedule of mystery. The schedule without rhyme or reason." He swished the mop back and forth, the triceps in his arm bulging. "Gotta love the schedule."

"Does that mean there's no chance of me getting regular hours?"

"Regular how?"

"I don't mean nine to five. But it would be nice to work the same shift consistently."

"Instead of working a different shift every time you're here?"

"Exactly."

Travis plopped the mop into the strainer, squeezing out the dirty water. "You are not the first associate to make this kind of request."

"And?"

"And you will not be the first associate not to get it."

"I see." Finished with the bananas, she took another sip of coffee. "And the reason would be…"

"Power. It's all about power."

Renee nodded. "So begging wouldn't help my cause?"

"Nope. Already tried it." Finished, he started pushing the mop bucket back toward the storeroom. "Give me a hand, would you? The delivery should be here any minute."

She followed him, waving at Billy and Zelieka, who were working opposite ends of the meat section, pulling codes. Their fingers flew as they checked dates and tossed out-of-date stuff over their shoulders into two waiting grocery carts.

"I'll never be that fast."

"Sure you will. Give it a few months."

As Travis had predicted, the truck was idling outside the back entrance. Travis pulled the chain that dragged open the back door, and cold air rushed in. Renee rubbed her arms, and waited while the truck driver lowered the first pallet on the ramp. Travis stepped on the loader and drove it up to the pallet, hooking the prongs into the lower section of the pallet and depositing it carefully onto the middle of the stockroom floor. He tore open a piece of plastic and handed the packing list to Renee. "Start checking this, would you?"

She stepped around the shrink-wrapped pallet, counting boxes and marking them on the list. The pallet was mostly produce. Four cases of salad mix, all types. Two crates of oranges. Two boxes of red peppers, one of yellow, one of orange. Three flats of strawberries, two of blueberries. She went through the list, stopping occasionally to cut through the shrink-wrap and double-check the number of boxes. Travis drove the two remaining pallets, and Renee continued checking the list.

"Got everything?"

"Yeah, except I can't find this case of red licorice." They both climbed around the pallets, until Travis pointed out the box, tucked under two large boxes of dried whole-wheat pasta.

"That's it." Travis signed a sheet on the driver's clipboard, and the two of them started breaking the pallet down, cutting away shrink-wrap and setting the various boxes on wheeled carts. Billy and Zelieka each grabbed a full cart and disappeared into the store to stock the produce section. Travis and Renee continued tearing apart the pallet. This was the most physical part of the job, and her back was sore from four days of labor in a row. She moved slowly, testing the weight of each box before she lifted it. She'd learned the hard way when she went to grab a box of canned soup, expecting it to be cereal.

"Ooof." She struggled a little bit with a box of jarred olives.

"You all right?"

She stood, rubbing her back. "Yeah. A little stiff, that's all."

He stepped over to her, pushing a cart at her. "Go ahead and start putting up this frozen stuff. I'll finish the pallet."

She started to protest but he interrupted. "Go on. I want everything up before we open anyway. We're short today on the floor."

She nodded, grateful to be done with the heaviest job of the day. Dragging boxes off the pallet was much harder than anything else she had to do—except maybe stocking wine. Who was she to argue?

She started out the sliding doors that led to the store proper. Travis's voice stopped her. "Hold up!" He stepped past her and picked out a pair of heavy yellow gloves.

"Save your fingers."

"Thanks." She tossed them on top of the boxes and pushed the cart out to the frozen section. This was her favorite job, except floating. With frozen, you didn't have to worry about pulling codes or reorganizing merchandise. You just put up what was new, and made sure it was in the right place. Sure, your fingers got cold after a while, but the yellow gloves helped. She finished stocking bags of tri-color peppers, frozen strawberries and raspberries, and goat cheese pizzas, and went back for a couple more cartfuls. By that time, it was time for the store to open.

Travis stopped by as she was putting away the rolling cart. "You mind starting on 3 this morning?"

"Sure. I'll be up there in a minute."

"Super. Thanks." He walked away, a slight limp to his stride, and she felt a flash of guilt. She shouldn't have let him take over breaking down the pallet. The associates were supposed to be willing to do any job from scrubbing the toilets in the bathrooms to bagging groceries to wrangling carts outside to blowing up balloons and handing them out to toddlers. No matter what you were doing, you were on your feet, and the physical nature of the work meant that everyone who worked there got fit, fast. She'd even seen Angel, who had no visible muscle, heft boxes of wine with no discernable effort.

Renee could tell she was gaining strength, but she was sore in a way she'd never been working at the mansion. She stretched briefly as she stood at the third cashier station. At least she had little time for daydreaming, and she liked it that way.

She spent most of the day at the register, the familiar ache creeping up her right arm by the time she was done. She punched out, paying for a couple of bananas, a loaf of bread, and frozen spinach enchiladas on her way out. Squinting against the glare of the sun, she waved at Travis, who was striding across the parking lot.

"Done for the day?"

"Yes, and I actually have a day off tomorrow!" She opened her car and leaned in to start it. "I like to let it warm up."

"Any exciting plans?"

"We'll see. I might go into the city."

"Oh yeah?"

"I've never been to the Art Institute," she said.

"I haven't either."

"Well, I majored in art and design."

"Oh, yeah. I think you mentioned that when you were trying to impress me with your ACT score."

She smiled, rubbing her hands together.

"What medium did you work in?"

She was startled by the question. "Well, I used to paint a little, but drawing has always been my favorite. Pen and ink stuff. I always felt a little removed from the canvas with a brush. Drawing is more immediate, you know?" She stopped.

"What?" He stepped over to take a cart from a woman in her 40s who had just unloaded her groceries. "What were you saying?"

"You know what? I'm freezing." She shivered to prove her point. "Can we talk about this another time?"

"Sure thing." Renee got into the car, and he pushed the door closed. "Enjoy your day off."

As it turned out, Renee didn't go to the Art Institute. She'd had good intentions. But the day had dawned bright and bitter cold, with a wind that took her breath away. The idea of driving to the city and parking, or taking the train in and making the short walk to Michigan Avenue, didn't seem worth a look at any of the numerous Picassos there. She'd go another day. A day it was warmer.

Which left the issue of what to do with the rest of her day. She'd already cleaned the apartment, but that took little time in a place so small. She didn't feel like reading. She didn't feel like watching television. What did she normally do on a Wednesday? That was easy. She was at work. She'd said she didn't mind working weekends and why should she? She'd been doing it most of her working life. But at the mansion, she'd worked weekends *and* during the week. Having Wednesdays (or Thursdays, or Tuesdays, or whatever) off felt strange. She'd spent so much of her time working she had no idea of what to do with her so-called free time.

She needed to get out, bitter cold or not. She could feel that creeping sadness trailing tendrils around the day, threatening to pull her under. She needed noise, activity, people, distraction.

So resolved, she ran out to start her car and let it warm up her car for a good fifteen minutes before leaving. She backed out and turned left, driving slowly. She could swing by Starbucks, or Caribou a little further up the road. She could go to Target and buy socks, underwear, and cleaning supplies. She could drive out to the multiplex and catch a movie. When was the last time she'd seen a movie during the day?

Come to think of it, when was the last time she'd gone to a movie alone? If it had been something that Lars didn't want to see, Mollie or Lissa would go with her. It was as simple as calling and asking. Lars' dad hadn't seen a movie since the 70s, at least according to Mollie, and she'd given up on going with him. She wouldn't have had to see a movie, either. Mollie was always up for lunch at an upscale restaurant when there wasn't an event scheduled at the mansion. She never let Renee pay.

"It's a business expense," she'd say. "Research for our menu." Mollie had an amazing memory for food. She could remember specific appetizers from years ago, down to the spices they contained. She'd been trying to educate Renee's palate, but Renee had never developed the ability to taste something and deconstruct it. She could identify certain spices — easy things like nutmeg and cumin and dill and oregano-but lacked the ability to duplicate the recipe later the way Mollie could.

Lissa had inherited her mother's palate and her ability in the kitchen, and Renee had always been jealous of that bond. Renee had grown up with a mostly-single mom, whose happiness was inevitably tied to the man of the moment. None of her mother's boyfriends or husbands had expressed any interest in parenting Lois' odd, quiet little girl who spent most of her time outside examining bugs — they never noticed she was drawing them.

Renee knew her mother loved her, but she also knew her mother didn't understand her. Lois had saddled her with the name Candy, after all — not even Candace but Candy — and always had seem surprised that she had created a child so different from herself. She certainly hadn't understood why Renee wanted to go to college — that was for rich kids — or why she would want to study art of all things. Renee had known that she couldn't count on her mom for help, so she'd focused on getting good grades in high school. Her grades and that stellar ACT score got her plenty of financial aid — at least enough for a cheap state school like Southern.

Her first act arriving in Carbondale was to finally drop "Candy" in favor of her middle name. Candy had been a kid. Renee was an adult. Or so she'd thought as an 18-year-old. Renee stayed in touch with her mom, but she preferred phone calls to visits. She figured her mom felt the same way.

A car honked behind her, and Renee jumped. She gave an apologetic wave to the driver behind her, who responded with a wave of his own, the middle finger salute. Renee felt her face flush and pulled away too quickly, the car slipping on the pavement. She changed lanes, and the late model truck behind her zoomed by.

She took a couple of deep breaths and then turned

right, heading for Colleen's. She noticed the Christmas decorations were finally gone, and the snow in the front yard was trampled. A small, lopsided snowman welcomed her with stick arms.

Colleen answered the door.

"Hey. I should have called."

"Why? We're always home." She moved aside. "Come on in."

Renee followed her in, reaching for Rose, who smiled and kicked. "I'll take her." She nosed Rose's fat little cheek, and Rose squealed, grabbing a fistful of hair. "Ouch!" Renee carefully unwound her chubby little fingers from the clump of hair. "Forgot about the kung fu grip."

"Now you know why moms have short hair," said Colleen, holding up the coffee pot.

"Sure. Thanks," she said, as Colleen poured her a cup and handed her the creamer. She idly flipped through the magazine sitting on the kitchen table. *"Jen says Brad won't love Angie fat!" "Jessica's new man!" "Katie's parents fear the worst!"* She saw Colleen had almost completed the crossword puzzle.

"Who's Jessica?" Renee waved a magazine at her friend.

"Jessica Simpson. She and Nick Lachey just broke up. Not that was any surprise."

"Why not?" Renee found a picture of this Jessica, who had honey blond hair, an enormous mouth, and wide-spaced eyes that gave her a vaguely alien appearance. She looked up at Colleen. "I mean, why wasn't it a surprise?"

Colleen took a sip of coffee. "People have been reporting their breakup for months. Supposedly she had a fling or two while she was shooting *Dukes of Hazard* and then he was caught making out with some college student."

Renee studied the photo. "She looks like a Barbie

doll."

"Well, she's worth 30 million, I just read."

"What? What does she do?"

"She sings, she's got a line of makeup, I think. She's been in a movie." Colleen shut off the coffeepot and sat down at the table. "She and Nick were on *Newlyweds*. Remember that? It turned into a big hit."

"Vaguely. Was it on MTV?"

"Yeah."

"Okay. I think Lars used to watch it. She's known for being stupid, right?"

"I don't know," said Colleen. "Some people think that's just an act."

"Stupidity usually isn't an act." Renee shut the magazine and sighed. "Sorry."

"What?"

"I'm cranky. Some guy gave me the finger on the way over."

"For what?"

"What kind of finger?" said Jordan, who had materialized at Renee's elbow.

"It's a mean thing people do when they're angry, honey," said Colleen. To Renee, she said, "What happened?"

"The light was green and apparently I didn't respond fast enough."

Colleen shook her head. "Welcome to the suburbs!"

"What does that mean?"

"I've gotten the finger more here than I ever did when we lived in the city. People think road rage is something that happens on the highway, but try driving around here. People blow red lights and honk their horns and flip you off just about every day."

Renee sat for a moment considering. "Really?" She shook her head. "I guess I feel better then. And here I was thinking I was special, getting the bird flipped at me."

Colleen grinned. "Sorry. You're not special."

Renee felt some nameless anxiety leave her. This was the Colleen she knew, not the brittle, touchy version she'd been seeing lately.

"I have an idea," she said. "You have any lunch plans?"

Colleen gestured at the kitchen. "Nothing other than what you see here. Peanut butter and jelly, most likely."

Renee stood up. "Why don't I go get us something gourmet for lunch. My treat."

"Are you sure?"

"Yeah, it'd be fun. I want to check out that Whole Foods anyway." Rose was getting antsy, twisting back and forth. Renee set her down and she crawled over to a stuffed elephant and began shaking it.

"Are you going to the fun store?" asked Jordan.

"He means the toy store," said Colleen. "No, Renee's going to the food store."

Jordan looked crushed.

"You want to come? You can help me pick out something for me and your mommy. Sound good?" She looked at Colleen. "That okay with you?"

Colleen nodded. "If you're up for it, sure. I'll get his coat and booster seat."

"Can I pick something for me?" Jordan looked up at her.

"Sure." Renee stood, and followed him to the front door. "I'm sure we can find something you'll like."

Colleen helped Jordan into his sneakers and winter coat, pulling a hat over his hair. "Keep your hat on. It's cold outside. And be a good boy for Renee, all right?"

He pushed the hat further back on his head. "I will."

"Promise?"

"I promise."

Renee shrugged into her coat. "All right then, little

man. Let's go get some lunch."

"I'm not a man! I'm a boy!" Jordan said as he buckled him into the backseat.

A distinction without a difference, thought Renee, but kept her thought to herself.

At Whole Foods, Renee picked out some hummus, tabouli, and chicken salad with dill from the deli section. She lifted Jordan so he could choose a couple of handfuls of green grapes and showed him how to twist the tie to close the bag.

"Now let's get some bread, and some wine for your mommy..." she looked down at Jordan. "What am I forgetting?"

"Cookies!"

Renee relented. He'd been so good, holding her hand in the parking lot, and staying next to her in the aisle. She'd offered to let him ride in the cart but he'd told her that carts were for babies.

"I'll tell you what. Come with me while we get the rest of this stuff, and then we'll go down the cookie aisle."

"And I can pick out any cookies I want?"

"Yes. But only one package. And you have to share them with your sister."

"Only Taylor. Because baby Rose is too little for cookies."

"That's right." Renee selected a loaf of crusty French bread and added a jar of black olive bruschetta to the cart along with a bottle of sauvignon blanc and a shiraz.

"All right, Jordan. Let's hit the cookie aisle."

Jordan walked down the aisle slowly, studying each package. Renee watched him, her fingers resting on the cart. He came running back to the cart, a bag of cookies raised above his head. The purple box had koala bears on it.

"What kind are these?"

She read the box. "Walnut and chocolate chip."

He looked up at her, reaching for the box. "Do I like those?"

"I don't know. Do you like walnuts?"

"I don't know," said Jordan uncertainly, still clutching the bag of cookies. His lip trembled and began to cry. "What if I get them and then I don't like them?" His voice rose to a wail.

"Hold on, hold on." Renee steered him down the aisle. "Come on, Jordy. Let's see if they have cookies without walnuts instead." She found a green box and held it up triumphantly. "Here you go!" She read the box to him. "Chocolate chip cookies. And no walnuts," she added.

"But I like this box!" Jordan wailed, crushing the box against his chest. "I don't want THAT box!"

Oh my God, thought Renee. Who is this kid? "I thought you said you didn't want the one with walnuts."

His face was red. "YOU SAID I COULD PICK! AND I WANT THIS BOX!"

Renee looked around, embarrassed. What would Colleen do?

A woman in her 50s walked by, giving Renee an understanding look. "It's a challenging age, isn't it?"

"Um, yeah." Renee reached for the cookies, but Jordan whirled away from her. "NOOOOOOOOO!" Surely his screams could be heard throughout the store. Maybe Colleen could even hear him at home.

"Jordan. Jordan!" Renee raised her voice. "Look at me! You can get that box, okay? Okay?"

Jordan kept wailing. "I want my mommy! I want to go HOME!"

"Okay, okay! We're going."

"I want my mommy! I want my mommy!"

A man in a green apron approached her. "Is everything all right here? Can I give you a hand?"

"I want my mommy!" Renee reached for Jordan's

hand, and Jordan pulled away from her.

"Where is your mommy?" the man asked Jordan. "Is she here in the store?"

"She's at home," said Renee. "He's my friend's son."

But the man ignored Renee. "Where's your mommy at? Do you know who this is?"

Jordan stopped wailing. "It's Rennie," he said, pronouncing her name like he always did. "Rennie."

"And you know Rennie?"

Jordan shifted the cookies under his arm. "Yes! She's mommy's friend!" He showed the cookie box to the man—a store manager, Renee guessed. "She's getting me cookies." He wiped his nose on his coat. "These ones."

Belatedly Renee realized what was going on. The manager was making sure she wasn't in the process of abducting a child. "Hey, look, I know him. His mom's my best friend." She dug for her phone, feeling her face flush. "Call her. I just ran out to get us lunch."

He looked at her, and then looked back at Jordan, who had sidled next to her, still clinging to his precious cookies. "No, that's all right."

Renee swallowed and nodded. "I'm sorry. I didn't realize he could get so wound up." She looked at Jordan, but didn't reach for him. She didn't want to set him off again. "Jordy, can we go home now and see your mom and baby Rose? And you can eat the cookies?" Sweat trickled down her back.

He nodded and handed her the box. "I want them now."

Renee ripped open the box and handed him three cookies, rushing toward the checkout line. By the time they walked out to the car, Jordan was humming happily as he chewed his walnut-laced cookies, completely unfazed. Renee, her heart still pounding, was anything but.

**Chapter 10
Colleen**

Colleen grimaced as she climbed out of the car. Her back was killing her. She bent over to unsnap the baby out of her car seat, and felt a flash of pain streak up her spine. She'd downed two Aleve with her morning coffee, but she still felt stiff and awkward, holding her body as if it might betray her. She eased Rose into her stroller, bending her knees and groaning a little from the effort. The baby laughed in response.

"You think that's funny? You think Mommy being in pain is funny?" Holding the stroller on either side, she pushed her body upward, holding her breath. Walking was manageable. Bending, twisting, lifting, and carrying—pretty much everything she did all day long—were barely so.

A woman leaving Starbucks held the door open for her, and Colleen smiled gratefully. The woman nodded, waving at the baby, who slapped her hands on the stroller tray in response.

"What a cutie!" the woman said, and Colleen thanked her. She ordered coffee and a blueberry scone. She sat down, pulling the stroller close to her, and dug a baggie of Cheerio's out of Rose's diaper bag, dumping some on her stroller tray.

Colleen shifted carefully and picked at her scone. She pulled her Day-Timer out of the diaper bag to make a list for the grocery store. She'd been carrying one of these since she started at her first job out of school. She'd been so compulsive about being organized then, setting daily, weekly, monthly, and annual goals, tracking her time on various projects, and even noting every expense for her budget. Her job now might not pay a six-figure salary, but it required the same kind of organization, planning, and record-keeping abilities. Too bad no one seemed to recognize that fact.

"Ba ba ba ba ba," said the baby, shoving another Cheerio into her mouth. It fell out, sticking to the drool on her lower lip like a button.

"Here, silly." Colleen reached out and placed the piece of cereal into Rose's mouth, who began working it with her gums.

A woman about her age walked over, carrying a baby bundled in a snowsuit on her hip, a cup in her other hand. She gestured at the empty chair. "Anyone sitting here?"

"No, go right ahead."

The woman set her coffee down and pulled off her own jacket before taking her son's snowsuit off. She struggled a bit with the zipper, but finally managed to pull out a very fat, round-faced baby.

"How old is...he?"

"Thomas Evan. He's three months." The woman settled against the back of the chair, holding her infant on her left side. She picked her up coffee cup with her right, leaning her head to the side to drink from the cup. Colleen smiled, watching her automatically put as much distance as possible between her baby and the hot liquid.

"How old is she?" Rose was watching the other baby closely, looking from him to Colleen.

"Rose Emily. She's eight months."

Rose pointed and squealed. "Ba ba ba ba ba!"

"Is she saying 'baby?'" The woman was impressed.

"I wish I could say she's a baby genius, but that's her usual babble."

The woman nodded, tugging at her Wisconsin sweatshirt. "Is she your first?"

"My third. And my last," she added.

"Three? Oh my God." The woman ran her hand over her hair. "I can't imagine. I'm hardly managing one."

"It gets easier. Is he a good sleeper?"

"Sleep? No, he's not a fan. He goes maybe three hours at a stretch. Afraid you might miss something, aren't you?" She looked down, jiggling the baby gently, and gently kissed the top of his bald head. Colleen recognized the look—besotted but overwhelmed.

"You know what helped with my three? I tried them on their stomach. All three were tummy sleepers."

The woman's blue eyes widened. "But that's wrong! You're always supposed to put a baby on his back!"

Ah, the smug certainty of the new mom. She'd no doubt read all the books from Dr. Spock to Terry Brazelton, and had all the answers already. The only problem was that the answers didn't apply to every baby, no matter how much you wanted them to.

"I know," said Colleen gently. "But my oldest was a terrible sleeper. She was up every hour, screaming. Finally one time when she was six weeks old, I tried her on her stomach. She slept for four hours the first time." She reached down to pick up a couple of stray Cheerio's. "I didn't want to do it, but what can I say? I was desperate."

The woman bit her lip. Colleen could see her debating between the ironclad back-to-sleep rule and the possibility of an extra hour—maybe two—of sleep. Colleen wished she could help her. Forget the books. They could offer advice, but nothing and no one could prepare you for making these kinds of decisions. "I don't know," she said slowly, looking at her son. "The risk of SIDS is higher for babies who sleep on their stomach."

"It's also higher for babies who sleep in warm rooms or who are overdressed," said Colleen. "Look, I felt the same way. But I was so exhausted!" The woman nodded.

"My mom's the one who suggested it. 'Who cares what the books say?'" said Colleen, imitating her mother. "'When you and your brother were babies, you slept on your stomachs every night and you were perfectly fine.'" Colleen rolled her eyes. "Another thing you'll find out about being a mom is that your mom is pretty much always right."

The woman smiled sadly. "I lost my mom two years ago." She kissed her son's head again.

"Oh, I am so sorry." Colleen didn't know what to say.

"Yeah. She had breast cancer, and I thought I was done grieving. Then he came along and now I miss her every day."

"I can understand that." Colleen glanced at her watch. Fifteen minutes before preschool ended. She started to gather her stuff. "I've got to pick up my son," she said. "I hope it gets easier."

The woman nodded. "Thanks. I hope so too." Colleen bent slowly to zip the baby's coat and pushed the stroller out of Starbucks. She glanced back as she left. The woman had set her coffee down and was sitting with her son on her lap, motionless.

She thought about her as she drove to the Y. She should have done something more. She could have introduced herself, maybe given the woman her phone number.

Colleen could remember the overwhelming fatigue she'd felt after having Taylor. Other women had warned her about how tired she'd be, but she hadn't been worried.

Her chronic insomnia meant that she'd learned to function—and function well—on a few hours of sleep. After a few nights of lying awake, her body's drive and need would kick in and she'd sleep soundly for seven, eight, even nine hours. The next morning she'd feel energized and appreciative of the night's sleep in a way that people who slept normally never did.

But this was different. After having Taylor, she was exhausted all the time with the kind of fatigue that makes your body hurt. She could handle the swollen breasts and tender nipples and sting of urine when she went to the bathroom. As time went on, her body started to feel more like her own, even if a somewhat softer, fleshier version. But she never felt rested. When she did manage to sleep, Taylor would cry, and Colleen would jerk awake with a start. Peter tried to help, but the bulk of the responsibility fell on her. It wasn't as if he could grow breasts, after all, and she wouldn't be giving her daughter every possible opportunity and health benefit if she didn't breastfeed.

Colleen had put a fresh cup of coffee into the refrigerator only to find it there an hour later. She put diapers on Taylor backwards. She locked the keys in the car with the engine running. One morning she discovered she was out of diapers and drove to the grocery store to get them—forgetting Taylor at home.

It would have been funny if it hadn't been so terrifying, not to mention proof of her inability to be a good mom. What kind of mother could forget her own child? She'd paid for the diapers, snatched them from the cashier, and sped home in a panic, picturing gas leaks, house fires, crazed lunatics breaking in and running off with her baby. She barely had shut off the engine before she'd thrown the door opening, taking the steps two at a time. Taylor was sleeping peacefully on her Winnie the Pooh sheets, her eyes closed, one arm thrown out to the side.

Colleen had grasped the rails of the crib so tightly she thought she'd snap them, her body slowly sliding down. She'd crawled on her hands and knees out of Taylor's room into the hall, and grabbed a towel from the bathroom so she could cover her sobs with it. She'd sat on the floor leaning against the toilet, her body shaking, her heart pounding. She wasn't sure how long she'd cried, or how long she'd sat afterwards. When Taylor had stirred, and then cried, Colleen had slowly pushed herself off the floor. She'd taken a deep breath as she stood looking at her daughter. Taylor had stopped in mid-cry when she'd seen her, her eyes wet and round. "Hi, little bug." Colleen had reached for her daughter, and fed her, and the day had continued. She was the only one who would ever know what had happened. She never even told Pete.

Certainly Renee wouldn't understand. The only person who might understand was her mother. Colleen had sent her home after Taylor was a week old, certain she could handle a newborn on her own, but after the diaper incident, she called her mother.

"Can you come?"

"Of course," her mother had said, all business. "I'll get a flight tomorrow."

The next morning, there she was on the doorstep. Colleen had been sitting on the couch amid a pile of baby laundry, and she had dragged herself up, walking slowly to the door. When she saw her mother's wide, lined face, she had started to cry. Her mom had hugged her.

"It's all right. I'm here." And she had stayed, and done everything. She'd shopped and cooked and cleaned the refrigerator and answered the phone and let Colleen sleep as much as possible. "I feel like I should be doing more," Colleen had said, watching her mother making homemade lasagna.

"You're doing the most important thing. You're recuperating from making a whole new person!" It was her mother who'd made her feel less guilty about using formula. She'd tried to nurse Taylor, but she had trouble latching on, and it was easier to use a bottle. "Oh for goodness sake, Colleen. Don't be so hard on yourself! Millions of babies have done just fine on formula. Including you and your brothers."

Colleen had wished for her cheerful certainty. Her mom had never seemed to question any of her parenting decisions. She would follow her lead. By the time her mother left eight days later, Colleen had felt some semblance of hope that she could manage parenting. She'd also realized on a visceral level how much her mother had loved her and her brothers. What she felt for Taylor, her mother had felt for her. That epiphany had deepened their not-always-close relationship, and she was the only person Colleen truly relied on for parenting advice. She couldn't imagine having to navigate the last seven years without her. But her mom lived across the country. Talking to her several times a week was only a temporary respite from the loneliness she often felt.

That's why she'd agreed to go to Melissa's book club, even if she was surprised by the invitation. She arrived at Melissa's three-story monster house a few minutes after 7:00 p.m., a copy of the book in her purse.

This wasn't the book club she was expecting. This was a full-on cocktail party. Hot artichoke dip with baby carrots, sliced red peppers, and cauliflower heads sat next to several kinds of Brie, mozzarella balls rolled in walnuts, and thin slices of prosciutto wrapped around honeydew melon. There were stuffed mushroom caps bulging with cheese and toasted breadcrumbs, grilled asparagus, toasted baguettes with caviar, and strawberries dipped in two colors of chocolate. Melissa would never serve anything as pedestrian as chips and dip, even at a casual get-together like this one. Her crystal stemware sparkled, and she had laid out cloth napkins. Cloth!

Colleen's own version of entertaining usually involved some variation of chili, chips and salsa, and beer, wine and maybe a few mixed drinks, served in plastic cups (green and red for the holidays; red, white, and blue for the Fourth of July). Here, there was a full bar with everything from mojitos to white Russians. For book club!

Colleen took a plate, choosing a selection of the most delectable looking treats, and sat down on the edge of one of the overstuffed couches, careful not to spill her apple martini. She smiled and said hello to several women she recognized, and settled down to eat. Once she did so, Colleen could see that her plate dwarfed the others. Women had placed peremptory appetizers on their plates—one woman had chosen three baby carrots with an almost imperceptible smudge of hot artichoke dip while another's held one tiny stuffed mushroom.

She chastised herself. How long would it be before she remembered that food was only for show at functions like these? You ate with your family, not at all-women parties. The hostess' job was to serve the most elegant, complicated, exotic menu, and the guests' job was to resist all but a tiny forced bite. Colleen ate quickly to hide her mistake. The stuffed mushroom was particularly good—a mix of sausage, spices, and breadcrumbs—and she made a note to ask Melissa for the recipe. Then she'd be able to eat more than one without feeling guilty.

A woman sat down next to her and Colleen looked up, surprised to see Amelia. "Oh, hi there!"

"Hello, Colleen."

"I didn't know you came to book club. This is my first time."

"Welcome." Amelia smiled briefly and took a sip of her red wine. Too bad, thought Colleen. She's still not pregnant.

"All right, ladies. Anyone need a freshen-up on their beverage before we begin?" Melissa stood, a copy of

Never Let Me Go in her hand. Colleen had started reading it three weeks ago, but she'd barely made it through the first couple of chapters. She'd started skimming it in haste last night, trying to figure out the major plot points without having to actually read the thing. Now she couldn't remember the names of the main characters or what had happened in the book. She figured out that the characters were clones or some other artificial humans, but after that the storyline got away from her.

She needn't have worried. After maybe five minutes of discussion about the ethics of cloning humans, the discussion devolved into problems with the basketball program for first through third graders at the Y.

"The coaches are pushing too hard," said one of the women, who Colleen recognized from Taylor's school. Her son was a year ahead of her. "It's not supposed to be about winning at this stage. The kids are supposed to be learning basic sportsmanship skills, teamwork, the fun of the game."

Most of the women nodded in agreement, but Melissa crossed her arms over her chest. "Wait a minute. These boys aren't in kindergarten. They can learn sports skills and still want to win. What's wrong with that?"

"Nothing's wrong with wanting to win. It's the single-minded focus on winning that I have a problem with. Last week, Kenny's team lost and now he doesn't want to play anymore."

"That's not the league's fault," said Melissa, leaning back in her chair. "Some kids aren't cut out for competition. Isn't it better to find that out now?"

Colleen looked from one to the other. The side conversations of the other women had died down, and the room was quiet except for muted jazz playing from the hidden speaker system. There was an unspoken but unbreakable rule among the moms. You never criticize a child who wasn't your own—at least not to the child's mother. Melissa was teetering on the edge of that rule.

"I don't think a second grader should be discouraged from competing in organized sports because his team isn't as good as another," said the woman. "Whether your team wins or loses is the luck of the draw anyway."

Melissa shook her head. "I don't see it that way. My boys have played in the league since they were four-year-olds and they love to compete. They want to win, and Gavin and I encourage that."

"They're children! Sports shouldn't be all about winning."

Melissa cocked her dark bobbed head to the side and shook it thoughtfully. "That's unrealistic. Life is about winning and losing. They're going to be competing in school, competing to get into college, competing for the best jobs. The more they do that early on, the better equipped they'll be when they get older. I can't imagine any of us," she gestured around the room, "want our children growing up without the critical skills they need to do well in the game of life."

Point and match, thought Colleen. Who was going to side against Melissa now? What parent didn't want her child to be as well-equipped, well-adjusted, and well-prepared for life as possible? After all, it was no longer acceptable to be a fair parent, even a good one. Now you had to be willing to go the extra mile. Some four-year-olds in Jordan's preschool class were already taking ballet and gymnastics and swimming and Irish step dancing. Their mothers dragged them from lesson to lesson, giving them every conceivable advantage, presumably.

Colleen had told Taylor and Jordan they could choose one activity at a time. For Jordan, it was basketball now, soccer in the summer. Taylor had started off in gymnastics but had decided Irish step dancing was the bomb. Colleen was sure it was because it was so noisy—and because Sasha had been taking lessons since she was three.

She turned toward Amelia to catch her eye, wondering what she thought of this conversation. Colleen's kids were competitive enough. She already had a hard enough time teaching them good sportsmanship, manners (punishing Taylor for telling another girl in her dance class that she wasn't as good as Taylor was), and all those so-called life skills Melissa was harping on.

But Amelia appeared to have tuned out the conversation. She was sitting with the book open on her lap, reading. Colleen nudged her.

"You're not supposed to be doing that, you know."

Amelia looked up at her, her expression blank. "Doing what?"

"Reading. A book. At book club."

There was a moment, and she smiled, closing the book. "I've only been coming for a few months. But there's been little discussion about the actual books."

Colleen shrugged. "I can't say. This is only my second time." She didn't add that it would probably be her last. She wanted to connect one-on-one with someone, not sit in a group and watch Melissa as alpha dog scare the rest of them into submission.

"Well, this is about my only social outlet besides yoga." Amelia set her still-full glass down, folding her hands in her lap. "I enjoy yoga more," she added in a low voice.

Colleen leaned forward. "You take yoga?"

Amelia nodded. "I teach, too. My yoga practice is all that's been keeping me sane."

Colleen nodded. "No luck getting pregnant yet?"

Amelia looked startled.

"Oh, I'm sorry," said Colleen, immediately mortified. "I just noticed the wine…"

Amelia lifted her hand. "You didn't say anything

wrong. And no, we haven't had any luck yet. Or I should say the only luck we're having is bad."

Colleen took another sip of her martini. "So, you're a yoga teacher?"

Amelia looked relieved at the change of subject. "Yes. I teach at a studio in the city."

"Oh. I didn't realize you worked."

Amelia laughed. "Well, the teaching is a new thing. I had taken a leave of absence and then my company laid me off. So I figured this was the time for me to pursue my passion. One of them," she added.

Amelia exuded something, Colleen thought. She exuded calm. Colleen herself felt anything but calm most of the time. Distracted, irritated, exhausted, overwhelmed, annoyed…no, calm definitely did not come to mind. Was it yoga or was it the fact that Amelia wasn't a mom? Was it both?

"Wow," said Colleen, immediately feeling like a moron. "You're lucky. I mean, to have something you love to do."

"I do love it. I'd had a regular practice for four years before I decided to take the leap and get certified as a teacher. Teaching has deepened my practice in a way I could have never expected. It's incredibly satisfying to help guide people on their yoga paths."

Surprisingly, Melissa turned the conversation back to the actual subject of the book, and their conversation ended abruptly. As they got up to leave, though, she grabbed the opportunity. "Amelia, I know you teach, but would you like to come over for coffee sometime? Maybe some morning you're home?"

Amelia pulled her coat tight and smiled. "Certainly. That sounds lovely."

Colleen mentally reviewed her calendar. "How about Friday? Ten-ish? Or whatever works for you."

"That would be perfect. I teach Friday afternoons,

so I'm free."

"Great! We'll see you Friday, then."

Pete didn't get it. "She's coming for coffee. So?"

"Don't you get it? I asked and she said yes." Colleen shook out her black slacks, lined up the seams, and hung them on the hanger. They were good for another day — or rather, another adult night out when no dirty little hands would grab them.

"I get it. I don't get what the big deal is."

Colleen sighed. She knew he didn't get it. Pete got his "people needs" met at work. "You're all I need, babe. You and the kids." Like most men she knew, he didn't think it was possible to spend all day with your children and feel lonely. Nor could he imagine that with all the women of similar age and circumstance in their very own neighborhood, she still didn't feel like she had a true friend, someone she'd gotten past the small talk phase with. She wanted someone like that. Someone like Renee — or the way things had been with Renee before.

Chapter 11
Renee

She'd hit a turning point faster than she'd expected. When she woke in the morning, she no longer had that feeling of momentary disorientation, opening her eyes to an unfamiliar ceiling, a white wall instead of the deep hunter green of the bedroom she'd shared with Lars. She made the drive to the store without thinking about it, and the apartment smelled familiar, not odd, when she came home.

In that sense, life was easier. This was normal then, the new normal. But now that her mental energy was no longer consumed by learning those oh-so-necessary Dave's skills—like punching in UPC codes at the register, separating refrigerated from non-refrigerated items while bagging, and learning the store layout so she could lead a customer to the exact item he or she was searching for, be it giant stuffed kalamata olives or soy Swiss cheese or Yogurt Honey Peanut Balance bars, thoughts of Lars were trickling in like dust in a poorly built trailer.

Making a radical change in your life is easy in that respect. You're so caught up in charting your new course, not to mention sticking to it, that you don't have a lot of time to consider the wisdom of your decision. It's only after the land you're traveling starts to look a bit more familiar, not so strange and off-putting, that you even have enough brain neurons available to ponder thoughts less pressing than will you be able to survive the journey.

Now Renee found herself with room to mourn. Of course the timing couldn't have been better, with Valentine's Day around the corner. Everywhere she went she was assaulted by decorations in pink and rosy red, the fleshy colors of the human heart. Fuzzy, cuddly-wuddly stuffed bears with garish red lace hearts, foil-wrapped chocolate roses, bags upon bags of conversation hearts. Even Dealin' Dave's provided no respite. They'd added a few Valentine-themed end caps, with chalkboard signs reading highly original messages like "Sweets for your Sweetie." Even the animal product aisle had chewy dog treats shaped like white and red hearts. Apparently the idea of a dog chewing on a heart didn't bother devoted pet owners.

"Can't the store boycott Valentine's Day?" said Renee, unloading boxes of cabernet. She was working on a display that let shoppers choose between cab, chardonnay, and merlot, and milk or dark chocolate nougat-filled hearts. She held up a bottle of wine in one hand, a bag of chocolates in the other. "One-stop shopping! Get your valentine drunk and fat in one fell swoop."

Travis laughed. "One fell swoop. See, that's how I know you've got a college degree. That impressive vocabulary."

"You know this isn't even a true holiday. It's an artifice created by Hallmark to sell cards, chocolate, and flowers, and to inspire smugness in happily coupled people and misery in those who are not."

"Why don't you tell me how you really feel, Renee. Don't hold back." Travis bent to cut open another case of wine, and Renee could see the muscles of his forearms bulge slightly. His arms were marked with a variety of small scrapes and scars. She had her own collection, the result of carrying boxes all day. Sure the box cutter itself was inherently dangerous. A handful of men had taken over planes with them, after all. But she hadn't known it was possible to be sliced open by the edge of an innocuous-looking cardboard box until it happened to her. His skin was darker than her own, without the winter pallor her own displayed, and his hands were broad, his fingers strong-looking.

"Well?"

"Huh?" She started, realizing she'd been staring.

"I'm waiting for you to tell me how you really feel about Valentine's Day."

She hedged a minute, then thought, what the hell. Denial can only go so far. "Let me be hypothetical for a moment."

Travis nodded. "Another college-educated word."

She nodded, reaching for another pair of wine bottles. "Hypothetically speaking, let's say I'm a woman. A woman in her thirties. And I'm single. Which is fine. Which is great," she added. "And this is the first Valentine's Day in years—oh, let's say close to seven years—that I have been single. Can you see that that situation might suck, hypothetically speaking?"

Travis nodded gravely. "Certainly. But why does it matter if you're a woman? Wouldn't the circumstance of being single after so long be painful regardless of gender?"

Renee thought. "No, it's worse for women. Women have biological clocks."

"Don't give me that. So do men."

"Oh, come on. Get real."

"Hey, men have a drive to procreate just like women do. How do you think the species has managed to survive all this time?"

"But it's a biological imperative with women."

He raised his eyebrows at "biological imperative," but let her continue. "Men can have a kid at 50, 60, 70.

Look at Anthony Quinn. He had a kid when he was 80 or something. You're not going to see an 80-year-old woman pushing out a kid."

"Don't take this personally as a member of womankind, but I don't think I would want to see that."

"Ha ha. My point is that if a woman is going to reproduce, she's got a smaller window of opportunity than a man does. Can we agree on that, at least?"

He nodded. "Does that mean you want kids?"

"We were speaking hypothetically," she reminded him.

He broke down a box, tossing it on the bottom of the cart, before reaching for the next. "Seems like an easy enough question to me. I want kids. Some guys don't."

"So why don't you have them yet?" She stood, watching him.

"Hasn't happened." He shrugged. "Course I'm pretty much to blame. But that's a long story for another time," said Travis, "hypothetically speaking."

"Travis, could you come to the front?" Zelieka's raspy voice sounded over the store intercom.

Saved, thought Renee. Besides, her desire to procreate wasn't appropriate workplace conversation now, was it? She felt a flash of irritation. He was her boss, after all. Where did he get off asking her something so personal?

She was starting to get to know some of the other employees at Dave's now, but with the exception of Travis, their conversations were the kind of employee-bonding she was used to after years of working in the service industry. You got to know people in fits and starts. She knew Zelieka was a single mom of two boys at home, that Angel was thinking about going to school to become a massage therapist, and that Billy lived with his parents and hated it. She forced herself to ask questions and made an effort to get to know the people she worked with. After all, they were the people she was spending most of her waking hours with.

But her conversations never went deeper than the unfair schedule or the obnoxious customer or the amazingly stinky diaper some thoughtless mother had left in the women's bathroom. They were surface conversations, and she wanted something more than that. Cut through all the small talk and drill down to something more meaningful, something of substance.

That was one of the things she missed about college. If she wasn't exactly surrounded by people of like minds, at least there were those who were interested in tracing Picasso's art through the Blue Period to his creation of Cubism or deconstructing the significance of DaVinci's *Mona Lisa* years before Dan Brown came along. She'd read *The Da Vinci Code* on Mollie's recommendation, but hated the way it had used art as nothing more than clues to a somewhat-interesting historical religious mystery. Still, she had to admit that it had forced her to take a closer look at *The Last Supper*, a painting she had never been particularly impressed with before.

DaVinci's genius was not as a painter, but as an inventor and scientist. He wouldn't have been surprised to find people flying in planes or replacing diseased hearts with healthy ones five hundred years after he lived. He would have been shocked—and Renee thought, amused—to learn that his simple portrait was now considered one of the greatest paintings of all time.

But talking about art dilutes its effect. Art shouldn't have to be discussed. Its effect should be visceral, whether it was an unexpected punch in the stomach or a growing awareness of an emotion—sadness, joy, rage, disgust—that hadn't been there the moment before.

She'd always been most impressed by the artists who weren't afraid to break from tradition to create something that no one had seen before. They had the gift of vision, and the willingness to learn and develop and hone the skills it took to express the vision. Impressionists like Renoir, Manet, and Monet had tried to capture light's influence on objects and faces in an entirely new way. Andy Warhol took a simple soup label and turned it from an everyday image to an iconic statement. Jackson Pollack poured, dribbled, and threw paint on the canvas. And Chuck Close demonstrated that a child's paint-by-numbers approach could create something startling and true, where each portrait became more than a sum of its parts.

She'd always thought of her own work—if she dared to call it that—as art on art. A reflective response, a way to take something you'd seen before, something you thought you knew, and make you look at it differently. Turn it around, turn it over, turn it on its head. She'd wanted to make people look twice with her work, make them react. Maybe even make them laugh.

One of the first cards she'd designed had parodied Raphael's chubby, thoughtful angels. Most people had seen the pair of cherubs, even if they didn't realize they were part of a larger painting (the Sistine Madonna) or recognize the work as Raphael, an Italian painter who lived during the Renaissance. She'd sketched the cherubs, careful to maintain their sweet, appealing appearance and then had added little red horns, masks and tails. She'd made two versions of the card; one said "Happy Halloween," the other, "You bring out the little devil in me." Was it a statement of man's dual nature, the ongoing struggle we each fight in determining right from wrong? Or was it simply a joke? Either way, it caught people's attention.

She couldn't imagine having a discussion of man's dual nature with anyone at Dave's—aside from Travis, however. But she'd still agreed to attend a party at Angel's house that night. Angel shared a house with four other 20-somethings, two of whom also worked at Dave's. It was her first social invitation since she started at the store, and she didn't want to say no.

"Can I bring something?" she'd asked Angel.

"We'll have a pony keg, but BYOB if you want something else." Angel rolled her eyes. "And keep a close eye on it. It tends to be a free-for-all once people get going."

Renee had nodded. Warm, flat beer from a pony keg wasn't appealing so she'd bring a bottle of wine just in case. She'd probably wind up drinking soda or water anyway. She chose a V-necked blouse with a geometric pattern of maroon and brown rectangles along with her favorite skirt, a chocolate-colored suede, dark brown tights and boots. It was the most dressed up she'd been since she moved here, but she welcomed a change from her jeans, T-shirts, and ubiquitous Dave's vest.

Driving to Angel's, she drummed her fingers on the steering wheel. Her stomach hurt. It was one thing to go to work, where she had tasks to keep her busy and small talk was simple. But a party was different. At the mansion, she could always start a conversation with a stranger, but it was always in the context of having something to do—wiping the bar, washing glasses, showing off the seven fireplaces of the mansion.

The key to small talk was to ask questions and keep the conversation moving forward by making the appropriate noises and responses. And on anything of importance—be it religion or politics, or in a town like St. Louis, sports—to carefully avoid offering an opinion of your own. It was easier at the mansion when the only opinion of hers people were interested in was whether the crab cakes were a better choice over the beef-filled taquitos, and whether it was appropriate to serve champagne before the initial wedding reception toast.

She glanced at her watch. It was after nine already. She'd give it an hour. If she wasn't having fun by then, she'd leave. She might need more human contact but she doubted she'd find the caliber of conversation she missed at this particular party.

Her first look around confirmed her suspicions. A group of eight or ten people were sitting around a huge round table that upon closer inspection revealed itself to be a huge varnished tree trunk stained with cigarette burns and drink rings. A bright blue plastic bong sat in the middle of the tree table, while another, this one orange in color, was passed reverently from person to person. Half-empty plastic beer cups were scattered over the table, and two makeshift ashtrays were filled with butts. The air smelled of cigarette smoke and the sweet, slightly rank smell of pot.

Angel waved at her without getting up. "Renee!" She gestured at the bong. "Wanna hit?"

"No, thanks." Renee shrugged off her coat, feeling overdressed and over-aged. Everyone in the living room appeared to be in their early to mid 20s, and they were wearing thermal long-sleeved tops, T-shirts, and hemp pullovers. Today's hippies, thought Renee — the difference being that the ones today had piercings, tattoos, and artfully streaked hair in addition to their laidback attitudes and leftish political leanings.

No one seemed too interested in talking politics, though. One guy wearing a "Question Authority" T-shirt (he probably thinks that's a new idea, thought Renee) was telling a rambling story about his drunken attempts to go cow-tipping at Northern Illinois, a college town west of Chicago.

"See, it comes down to physics, you see?" He held his hands up. "It's not so much the amount of force you apply to the cow as it is where you apply the force, see? You need to apply the force to this one particular section of the cow's hindquarter to get serious tipping potential."

"Cow tipping is an urban myth, dude," said the guy sitting next to him. "It's like that story about the babysitter who keeps getting calls, saying 'have you checked the children,' and she's getting more and more freaked out and the dude keeps calling and she finally calls the police and they trace the calls and they say 'the calls are coming from inside the house!'"

One girl screamed but the others didn't look impressed.

"Joel, that's a movie. I just saw the trailer for it."

Joel was adamant. "Dude, it's a movie *now*. But it's based on an urban myth! The urban myth of the babysitter getting those calls."

"But that happened to me!" said Angel, sitting up. "I was babysitting and I kept getting calls on my cell and they kept hanging up, you know? I was totally freaked."

"So what happened? Who was it?" asked the girl who had screamed.

"It was my cell, dropping calls," said Angel, reaching for the bong.

There was a brief pause and then the group started laughing. "Fascinating story, Angel baby," said Dylan, the much-tattooed Dave's associate. "Scared the shit right out of me."

Renee sidled out of the room, her bottle of cool water in hand. In the kitchen, she found Travis talking with several lanky young men in their 20s.

"Renee!" He smiled, waving her over. "Come join us." He looked her up and down. "Decided against the Dealin' Dave's standard uniform, I see. Is this your non-associate look?"

"Um, yeah." She nodded, waving the wine bottle. "You happen to know where I could find a corkscrew?"

"You look nice." He turned and pulled open a drawer. "Hang on. I'll get it for you."

"I don't mind." She reached for the corkscrew, belatedly hearing the compliment. "Oh. Thanks!"

He didn't release the corkscrew. "Let me do it.

Years of practice, you know." He pulled the bottle from her grasp, glancing at the label. "Not a beer fan?"

She shook her head, indicating the bottles of water all three were holding. "Nor are you guys, it looks like."

"Oh, this is Sean and Damon." Both nodded at her. "They're in training. They're not allowed to drink."

The young men exchanged a look while Travis deftly pulled the corkscrew from the bottle. "At least not in front of their coach." Travis opened a cabinet and pulled down a wine glass.

Renee looked at Travis in surprise. "What kind of coach?"

"Cross country in the fall, and track in the spring. I work with the distance guys like these two."

Sean nodded. "Yeah, he tells us what to do and then goes on and on about how hard he trained in college."

Damon chimed in. "'I was doing 90-mile weeks my freshman year! This is nothing!'" He looked at Renee. "Yet he claims he can't run with us anymore. You know, his bum knee."

Renee looked from them to Travis, who simply grinned and shook his head. "Kids these days," he said to Renee. "Just don't have that work ethic."

"Oh yeah, you mean when you were out racing those dinosaurs, right?" Damon snickered.

"Yeah, doing speed work to escape the velociraptors."

Travis turned back to Renee. "They like to make me feel like an old man."

She nodded, and indicated the wine bottle. "Join me?"

He shook his head. "No thanks." He held up his water bottle. "I'm good."

"Hey, T, we're gonna jet." Sean crunched the plastic water bottle he was holding. "See ya later." The two nodded at Renee and left.

The house was a small one, and smoke had started drifting into the kitchen. Renee waved her hand. "Is there anywhere else here we can stand?"

"You mean where you won't leave reeking of pot smoke? Probably not." But he motioned her toward the back of the kitchen, where a collection of mismatched chairs sat around a round, oversized table. A few bowls of chips and corn chips sat on it but looked like they'd been ignored. At least until the munchies struck, thought Renee.

"Party snacks?" He pushed a bowl in her direction.

"No thanks." She took a sip of wine. "So, is that a problem for you?"

"What's that?"

"The pot smoking in the living room? I don't recall a question like that on the Honesty Index."

He shrugged his shoulders. "As long as they're not showing up stoned at work, it's their prerogative."

"But you don't want those guys drinking."

He shrugged. "That's different. They're athletes. And more importantly, I'm their coach."

"How did you get into that?"

He leaned back in his chair, stretching his legs out. "A long time ago—not as long as they'd have you believe, though—I ran in college. Tore my medial meniscus my senior year. I had surgery but that was the end of my running career. When we first moved out here, we lived near the college, and I saw the team training all the time. This is my fourth year."

She noticed the "we," but let it go. "Do you run with them?" That would explain why he always looked so tan, even in the middle of winter.

"No, those days are gone. I'll go out on training runs on my bike, though. Whip them with encouraging words."

"So that's why you work a split shift so often."

A smile crossed his face. "During the season, I do.

117

Otherwise I prefer to work nights, have the days to myself."

Renee didn't say anything for a minute.

"What?"

"Nothing. I just think it's cool that you're a coach."

"Cool, huh?"

"Shut up. I just read that 'cool' has actually stood the test of time as slang meaning, well, cool. It's showed remarkable longevity."

"What hasn't? Stood the test of longevity?"

"Let's see." She squinted, trying to remember. "Rad. Far out. Groovy. Neat. Keen. Awesome. Oh, and bad."

"Bad meaning good."

"Exactly. There are more, but I can't remember."

"Think we could bring some of them back? Groovy and far out have much more appeal than something weak like cool."

"I don't know. What sociological impact can two little people make in the world?"

"'We must be the change we wish to see in the world,'" he quoted, watching her.

She nodded. "Gandhi."

"Very good."

She shook her head. "What is this, a quiz?"

"You're the one who's always bragging about her impressive math skills," he said. "I'm trying to explore the breadth of your liberal arts education." He was leaning against the kitchen table, one leg crossed over the other, his body relaxed. She tried not to notice the lean muscles in his arms.

She looked at him without speaking. She was aware of the noise from the living room, laughter mixed with Coldplay, the faint odor of cigarettes and marijuana, the slight rustle of her skirt as she shifted her weight. She felt a flush spreading over her face and wondered if he knew what she was thinking.

They continued to look at each other, and Renee was sure. He might not know exactly what she was thinking, but the attraction wasn't in her mind. He felt it too.

Chapter 12
Colleen

Colleen heard the doorbell and debated not answering. Crud. It could be important. She tucked the magazine she was reading back on the pile. She could catch up on Brangelina later.

Renee was at the door, wearing her winter coat over her Dealin' Dave's vest and baggy jeans. She held up a paper bag with the DD logo, a fat, satisfied-looking parrot. "I brought treats!"

Colleen peeked inside the bag. "Sweet or salty?"

"Both, of course." Renee pulled out a bag of blue corn chips, a plastic tin of hummus, and meringue chocolate cookies. "Have you tried these?" she said, opening the cookies. "They taste like air at first, but they're sort of addictive."

Colleen took one. It melted on her tongue immediately, leaving a vague cocoa taste. She tried another, wiping the powdered sugar from her fingers.

"What do you think?"

"Dusty. They're all right, I suppose."

"Only 25 calories each! And we have lemon, orange and vanilla too!"

"Haven't you punched out for the day?"

Renee laughed. "Point taken." She tore open the bag

of chips. "Besides, we're supposed to try all the new products so we can make 'authentic recommendations' to customers." She held up her fingers to make little quote marks. "You know, as opposed to the inauthentic recommendations I usually offer."

"Do you have to do that?"

"Let's just say it's highly suggested," said Renee. She dipped a chip in hummus. "Col, try this. It's got chili peppers in it. It's amazing." She looked up at Colleen. "Besides, I don't mind. It's fun knowing what we sell. It's not that different from what I did at the mansion. Salted versus unsalted almonds, which kind of cracker goes best with this kind of cheese, what wine to serve with different courses, that kind of thing." She sat down at the kitchen table, tucking one leg under her.

"You like it." Colleen felt a flash of irritation. "Still, it's not exactly a career." She hated how her voice sounded, but she couldn't help it.

Renee flushed slightly. "I do! I like selling groceries. What can I say? It's not like it's forever." She looked around. "Hey, where is everyone? Your house is so quiet."

"Pete's off today. He took the kids to the Y."

"Rose too?"

I said the kids, didn't I? Colleen shrugged. "Yeah." She watched as Renee got up and poured herself a glass of water from the sink. Colleen picked up another cookie, taking a contemplative bite.

"Am I interrupting you or something?" said Renee suddenly. She was still standing at the sink, her glass in her hand.

"What? No. No. Why would you say that?"

Renee looked at her water glass. "You just don't seem like you want company, that's all."

Colleen didn't say anything for a moment. Well, she didn't. But Renee wouldn't understand that an afternoon to herself was as rare as a Hollywood starlet without veneers. She had promised Pete that she wouldn't use the time to catch up on errands sans kids or do laundry. She'd sat her kitchen table for a few minutes, listening to the soft swish of the dishwasher. The quiet started to feel oppressive, and a feeling of sadness had started to steal over her. She had looked around the kitchen. Forget what she had told Pete. She should be making a grocery list. Folding the towels in the dryer. Sweeping up the bits of food under the baby's high chair. She could count seven different things she needed to do in this room alone. How could she simply sit here and waste this time?

Colleen had gotten up and dug in her stack of magazines, looking for something she hadn't read. She'd dug up an old *Enquirer* and within minutes had lost herself in the steamy details of Lindsay Lohan's parents' divorce case. Until Renee had shown up. But that wasn't Renee's fault.

"Look, it's not you. I'm just in a mood."

Renee immediately slid into the chair across from her. "Why? What's the matter?"

Colleen set the cookie down. "I don't even know if I can answer that question."

Renee licked the salt off a chip, watching her. "Is it Pete? Is it the kids?"

Of course that was all it could be, right? What else did Colleen have going on? Aloud, she said, "No. It's not them." She reached for a coffee mug for Renee, grimacing a little. Her back still was bothering her, even though she'd been popping Aleve every day. "Maybe I wish it was Pete or the kids." She gripped her coffee cup in both hands. "Gosh, I don't mean that. That's the last thing I want. I seem to be easier at solving their problems than my own."

"You mean it's easier to tell someone else what to do than to tell yourself," said Renee. "I have known you since college, remember."

Colleen forced a smile. "Point taken."

"Because you have blinders when it comes to yourself." Colleen looked up with a frown and Renee held up her hand. "Not just you. We all do. It's a million times easier to figure out what someone else's issue is and how to fix it than to help yourself with your own. That's why doctors aren't allowed to diagnose themselves with an illness."

"They're not?"

Renee shook her head, confident as always. "Huh uh. Look at me and Lars." She gestured. "You can tell me. You knew all along he wasn't going to marry me, didn't you?"

Colleen hesitated. "Not all along. Maybe after the first year or two, though, yeah."

Renee sighed. "There you go. And I only figured it out after he actually told me. See what I mean? I had what they call selective blindness. Failing to see the obvious when it's in front of my face." She ate some hummus.

"You miss him."

Renee shut her eyes, leaning her head against the kitchen chair. "I do. But not as much as before." She drank some coffee and then held up her cup. "Progress!"

Colleen changed the subject. "So, what's the latest with the guy from work? The assistant manager?"

"Travis." Renee pulled her hair out of its ponytail, running her fingers through it absently. "And the latest? Nothing. And definitely something."

"How's that?" Colleen had seen him at Dealin' Dave's a few times, and he was attractive, in a skinny kind of way. He did always seem to be in a good mood. It had to be an act.

"There's *something* between us. I'm sure I'm not so desperate I'm imagining it. But where does it go from there? He works at least 50 hours a week, he coaches a college track team, and I work some nights he doesn't. The situation doesn't exactly lend itself to a budding romance."

She sighed. "Besides, he's my boss, technically. I'm not sure if he's even allowed to date anyone at the store."

Colleen nodded.

"Besides, it's a proximity thing. For all I know, we don't have anything in common other than Dave's. Not a great foundation for a relationship, right?" She ate a couple of chips.

Colleen didn't believe her, but she let it drop. It wasn't like Renee needed to jump back into a relationship right away anyway.

"Besides, what if Travis and I do hook up and it doesn't work out? Didn't I just learn that particular life lesson the hard way?" Renee mused out loud.

Colleen put her cup down. "Yeah, you did. And why would you want to jump into a relationship anyway? Look, Renee, you've got an opportunity here. You don't have to think about anyone but yourself. You could go back to school! You could travel. You could do whatever you want, without having to take one single person's thoughts or feelings or needs or wants into consideration. Why would you want to give that up so quickly?"

"I'm not saying I want to give that up. I'm just saying it would be nice to have someone to talk to again. Besides you," she added.

"I'm only saying it wouldn't kill you to be single for a while," said Colleen. "If I were you..."

"But you're not me." Renee gestured at the kitchen. "You've got it all already. What's wrong with me wanting that too?"

"Absolutely nothing," said Colleen. She knew Renee would never understand that you could have it all—and want nothing more than to escape it. She wondered if Amelia would be like that, too, and briefly considered cancelling their coffee date. But that would be rude. Still, she felt a flash of worry. Amelia probably wouldn't even like her. Get a grip, she told herself. She accepted your invitation. It'll be fine.

That Friday morning, Jordan held up the spoon he was holding to show Colleen. "Like this, Mommy? Mash them like this?"

"That's perfect." Colleen bent over and moved his hands a little higher on the spoon. "See, it's easier if you hold it up here. See?"

"Uh huh." He continued mixing the bananas into the rest of the batter, flour drifting out of the bowl. Colleen didn't say anything; she'd wipe it up when they were finished. She let Jordan put muffin wraps into the tins, and then showed him how to scoop out spoonfuls of batter into each wrap. He spilled batter with each attempt. It would have been easier to simply do it herself, but when Jordan had seen her turn on the oven, he had insisted on "helping."

By the time the muffins were in the oven, though, he'd lost interest in the project and had returned to playing with the mound of Legos in the family room. The baby was still sitting in her high chair, which gave Colleen an opportunity to wipe up the counters and do a quick damp mop of the floor.

Amelia should be here any minute, just as the muffins would be ready. I hope she's not allergic to nuts, thought Colleen suddenly. She should asked; she could have left the walnuts out of the recipe. Oh well—too late now.

When the doorbell rang, Jordan jumped up. "I'll get it!" He pounded down the hallway, and Colleen followed. Amelia stood on the doorstep, holding a foil-wrapped plate.

"Hi! I'm so glad you're here! Come on in," said Colleen, stepping back into the house.

"Hello, Colleen. And hello--," she waited for his response.

"Jordan," he said, his hands behind his back.

"He's shy around strangers," said Colleen. "He'll warm up to you."

"Oh, that's all right. I'm shy with strangers, too," she said to Jordan, who looked skeptical and ran back down the hallway to the family room.

"Chocolate chip and pecan cookies," said Amelia, offering Colleen the plate.

She peeled back the foil, relieved to see the nuts. "Ooh, these smell divine. Thank you."

Amelia followed her into the kitchen. "I love your cabinets. Are they new?"

"Thank you," said Colleen. "We had them done last year."

Amelia sat at the end of the table, and Colleen carried the coffee over to them. "Another minute or two and I'll have muffins ready."

Jordan slammed two pieces of Lego's together. "Bam! Bam! Crash!"

"Jordan. I've got an idea. Why don't you play downstairs?"

He started to whine. "I don't wanna play downstairs."

"All right. How would you like to watch a video?"

"Can I watch *Full House*?" Taylor was obsessed with reruns of the sit-com and now Jordan wanted to watch it all the time, too.

"If you agree to watch it quietly while Mrs. Nelson and I talk in the living room," said Colleen. She looked at the baby, debating, and then extracted her from the high chair. Better to bring her with where she could keep an eye on her.

The oven dinged, and Colleen set Rose on the floor while she pulled the muffins out. "Honey, your muffins are done!"

Jordan didn't even turn his head.

Colleen made a quick plate, picked up her coffee,

and directed Amelia to the living room. "I'll be right back," she said, returning with the baby on her hip. She started screeching, bouncing on Colleen's hip.

"She thinks this is a great ride," said Colleen, smiling at Amelia. Colleen sat down on the edge of the couch, the baby on her lap. She took a careful sip of coffee, away from the top of her head. When the baby squirmed, Colleen let her slide down onto the floor.

"She's at that growing-independent stage," said Colleen. "You know, where they don't want you to hold them unless they *want* to be held."

Amelia nodded, glancing at Rose, who had crawled over to investigate the lace of her shoe.

"She likes laces," said Colleen, master of the obvious. "So, I'm so glad you accepted my invitation!" She could have added how excited she was to get to know her better, how she'd been hoping they'd click the way she and Renee had originally. Just add water. Instant friend. But it wasn't a good idea to come off as too needy. For all she knew, Amelia wasn't interested in becoming friends. But then why would she have accepted the invitation? "So, how long have you been in the book club?" She jumped up and grabbed the baby, who was shoving some pillow fringe into her mouth. Another choking hazard she'd never noticed before.

"Several months. Though I'm not sure I'll stick with it." Amelia pulled her muffin apart into two neat halves. "There doesn't seem to be much discussion about the actual books we're reading."

Colleen laughed, then covered her mouth. "I'm sorry. I'm not laughing at you. It's just that's pretty much par for the course. Whether it's book club, Bunco, Pampered Chef parties…conversation devolves into talking about the kids." She caught herself. "Oh, I'm sorry."

Amelia lifted her hand. "No apologies. I've noticed

that myself, believe me." She put a neat piece of muffin in her mouth. "I was in a book club at work," she offered suddenly. "We'd take a Friday lunch once a month. Gave us something to talk about other than work—at least that was the theory." She shrugged. "Our conversations devolved, too, into talking about work."

Colleen jumped up again to rescue the baby, who'd become stuck between the end table and the wall and was starting to howl. "I call it the lowest common denominator effect," she called over her shoulder as she hurried into the family room with Rose on her hip. "Jordan, would you watch your sister for one minute?"

He didn't answer, mouth open, eyes fixed on the television. Colleen snapped her fingers and raised her voice. "Jordan!"

He turned his head toward her, mouth still open, eyes dull. "Huh?"

"Watch your sister. I'll be right back."

She found the playpen in the basement and dragged it upstairs, positioning it in front of the couch. "Now I can't see!" whined Jordan. Colleen pulled the playpen to the side, threw a handful of toys in, and plopped the baby into it. "There. Now you're both fine."

She sat down on the couch in the living room and exhaled.

"Lowest common denominator?" prompted Amelia.

"Oh, right. I mean, you wind up talking about whatever topic the group has in common. Around here that's husbands and kids."

Amelia nodded thoughtfully. "I never thought it like that, but you're right." She rotated her shoulders in a graceful move. "Even at yoga, we all wind up talking about...yoga."

Colleen felt a sudden flush of pleasure. "Tell me more about how you got into yoga," she said, then hated the eagerness in her voice. Don't try too hard, Colleen, she reminded herself. Desperation is not becoming.

"I struggled with anxiety for years," said Amelia. "It started when Dan and I first got married. Initially I thought it was adjusting to being a newlywed. Then I thought it was the stress of moving too much, of living overseas. That was even before we started trying for a baby," she added, sitting back and tucking her left leg under her slim thigh. "Finally I realized it was *me*. I started reading about ways to treat anxiety and kept coming back to the fact that exercise is one of the most effective ways to manage it." She made a face. "That wasn't appealing, but then I started reading more about yoga, and the mind-body connection, and decided to try it." She laughed. "What can I say? I got hooked right away. Now if I'm not able to practice for at least an hour or two every morning, I don't feel like myself." She exhaled.

Colleen imagined having an hour (minimum!) to herself every day. Or tried to imagine it. That was pretty much outside the realm of her reality, at least for now. Her "free time" was spent catching up on laundry, paying bills, making grocery lists...and reading trashy magazines, she admitted.

"Does yoga help—with getting pregnant?" Colleen asked, and then immediately regretted it.

But Amelia didn't seem bothered. "It's supposed to, yes, even if it hasn't for me—yet, anyway." She inhaled and exhaled before she continued. "I'm working on letting that go. Not that I don't still want a baby. I do. But the yoga practice has helped me quiet that constant internal chatter—Buddhists call it 'monkey mind'—and live in the moment more. I haven't given up on getting pregnant, but I realized I was wishing my life away. Every cycle that didn't work, I'd want to speed up time so we could try again. That's no way to live, always pining for the future."

Colleen nodded, thinking of the many times she'd wished the kids were older—so they'd be sleeping through the night or potty-trained or able to communicate what they wanted or just not be so incredibly demanding. Counting the months or the years until she could go back to work, recover her adult self. And where had it gotten her? Taylor and Jordan were children now, no longer toddlers who commanded her attention every single minute. Even Rose was becoming a little girl, shedding some of her infant self with every new skill she mastered.

Colleen said, "I'd never guess *you* were an anxious person."

"I am, believe me. But yoga has changed how I react to the world," she said. "I sometimes say it makes me feel like I'm moving with the world, not swimming against it." She smiled. "Sorry. I'm not trying to evangelize. I know not everyone is a yoga junkie. Other than Dan, though, it's the one thing I can't imagine living without."

Colleen didn't have to imagine what she couldn't live without. Pete. The kids. Her mom. Renee. She had so much. Why couldn't she embrace what she had with the grace Amelia did? She nodded. "I have to tell you I'm envious of you," she said.

"Me?" Amelia laughed. "Please."

"You're so...serene." Colleen gestured toward the family room, where the TV was blaring. "I'm anything but. I feel crazed most of the time."

Another woman would have commiserated, and they would have bonded, even briefly, over the shared insanity of their stay-at-home-mom existence. Amelia didn't. "Why? Why do you feel crazed?"

And Colleen struggled for an answer.

Chapter 13
Renee

Renee's cell phone rang just as she was finishing dinner, yet one more frozen concoction from Dealin' Dave's. Forget cooking. Now she just plopped the plastic packaging onto a plate, and sat on her cool new couch with a towel on her lap, and ate while watching *Seinfeld* reruns or VH1, depending on what time it was.

She picked up the phone and saw "Lars/cell" on the screen, debated, then answered.

"Renee? Hey. Hang on." She heard the background noise abruptly stop. "Had to mute the game."

She didn't say anything. He'd been calling her every week or so, but she still felt a little twist in her heart when she heard his voice.

"Hi. What's up?" Her voice sounded perfectly neutral.

"Nothing. Checking in, seeing what's up."

Has he lost his mind? Aloud she said, "nothing much. Everything's good here."

"Yeah? That's good." He paused. "Hey, have you talked to my mom lately?"

"No. Why? Is everything all right?" she added, worried.

"Everything's fine," said Lars. "She's worried about

131

you, though. you, though."

"I've talked to her."

"Well, you know how she is. She misses you," he added.

"I know. I miss her too. And you," she added without thinking.

"Yeah, me too." Lars sighed. "Ren, you know I didn't want things to work out this way."

"We've covered this already." They'd had several conversations hashing over the end of their relationship. Each had started out as a neutral, objective, mature discussion. And each had wound up with Renee accusing Lars of lying to her. She still thought that he'd known all along he didn't want to marry her, and had strung her along, though she hadn't been able to bring herself to use those words. He insisted he hadn't known that until right before he told her so.

"I hear you." Lars sighed. "Look, my mom's still pissed at me. So call her, all right?"

"Pissed at *you*? Her favored son?" Renee laughed, not unkindly. "That's a new one."

Lars sighed. "Yeah, well, believe it. She let me have it the other night. Said that she thought you being gone would make me realize what a special person you are. That someone like you doesn't come along every day. That I'm basically an idiot."

She doubted Mollie would have called Lars an idiot, but Renee said nothing.

"You know what, Renee? If I could have, I would have. I swear. But every time I thought of being married, I felt...I don't know."

"Trapped?"

"Yeah. Trapped," he said. "I can't explain it. But it wasn't me. Even with you," he added. "If it was anyone, it would have been you."

Renee said nothing, pinching her nose hard. "You

don't have to say that."

"It's the truth," he said. "If it matters."

"It does," she said, her voice small. "Thanks. For telling me that."

Lars cleared his throat. "Call my mom, though, will you?"

"And let you off the hook?"

"Yeah…yeah, if you want, that would be good, too."

"We'll see," she said. "How's Speak Up going?"

"Not bad," he said. She could hear the relief in his voice that they had moved on to a less loaded topic. The website sales have really taken off, and I'm talking to some chains about carrying some of the shirts."

"That's great." Renee sat back down on the couch. "Were you able to get that additional financing?"

"Not from Charter Bank, but I did manage to swing an SBA loan. Originally I thought I'd need five years to pay it off, but the way things are going, I may beat that by a couple of years."

"What about the women's cut shirts? Did you decide to go with them or not?"

"You were right. I found a wholesaler and we made them an option for the five most popular shirts, and they've been selling like crazy."

Renee smiled despite herself. "Told you."

"Well, I've never had a problem taking advice from smart women."

They continued talking about his business for a while before she made an excuse to get off the phone.

"It was good talking to you, Renee," said Lars.

"You too," she said. "Take care." She hung up, then sat looking at the phone in her hand for a few minutes. For the first time since she'd left St. Louis, she'd been able to talk to him without getting angry, accusatory, or frustrated. What was left was only a creeping sadness that was worse when she was alone.

She was relieved, then, that she was scheduled to work the next five days straight. She welcomed the distraction. She even volunteered to work late when one of the high school kids who worked afternoons didn't show up the next day.

"Are you sure? You've already been here seven hours," said Travis, scanning the store. There were three employees working the registers, but at least four customers in every line — many with full carts.

"I wouldn't offer if I didn't want to," said Renee, stepping over to bag for Angel. "Just say you want me to stay and I will."

He turned to untie a balloon from one of the registers and offer it to a little boy. "If you want to stay, that would be great. You're not opening or anything tomorrow, are you?"

Renee was shaking out a bag to slide it into another one. "Hey, I'm thoughtful, not crazy." She finished loading the groceries and carefully set the last bag into the cart. "I put your cold stuff in one bag; the rest of it's in the other one."

The woman glanced at the cart. "Oh, thank you! I appreciate that."

"No problem." Renee was already sorting groceries to bag them as Angel scanned them, making small talk with the next customer in line. She'd rather be here, her hands and mind occupied, than at home anyway. There was something to be said for physical menial labor. Her right arm and shoulder had become used to the continuous motion of pulling groceries across the scanner, and she noticed she could lift a box of wine without straining. Her back and legs no longer hurt at the end of a day, replaced by a pleasant sense of exhaustion. And who said she had to dash home right after work? She sometimes sat and ate dinner in the break room, reading the remnants of the

Chicago paper or whatever magazines happened to be lying about.

"You still here?" Travis remarked one night. Renee and Zelieka were eating some stoneground corn chips with roasted corn and mango salsa that had been left out for everyone to sample.

"I'm on break," said Zelieka, checking her watch. "But I'm happy to go home. Say the word."

"Not you." Travis stuck a chip in the salsa and sampled it. "Your partner in crime here."

Renee had her feet up on the chair across from her. She had been listening to Zelieka talk about her kids. It had been a one-sided conversation; all she had to do was nod and make understanding noises occasionally. From what she could tell, Zelieka's two boys were what someone who euphemistically call, "a handful." Renee had wondered how she could even afford daycare for them on the hourly wage she made, but it turned out that Zelieka's mom watched (and spoiled) them.

"Can't get enough of this place, huh? Or are you gunning for my job?"

"Hardly." But Renee bit her lip, embarrassed that he had noticed her reluctance to leave. She started to get up. "Anyway, I was just leaving. Good luck with Lincoln, Z. I'm sure it's a phase. My friend Colleen has three kids and she says the year between two and three is the hardest."

"Hand to God, I hope you're right," said Zelieka, smiling. Renee pushed the chair back under the long table and headed for the break room door. Travis glanced at her face, then reached out to touch her arm as she walked by. "Hey, I'm joking. Don't leave on my account."

She shrugged. "I was just getting ready to go anyway. I've got lots to do tonight."

She could feel his eyes on her as she shrugged into her coat and left. It was bitter and still outside, her breath making dense little clouds. She started her car and sat there for a moment while it warmed up, grateful it was dark outside. What did he care if she wanted to sit in the break room for an extra few minutes? She'd felt unwelcome at Colleen's house the last time she'd seen her. Now she wasn't even welcome at work. Renee swallowed hard and blinked back tears before putting her car in reverse to drive home.

Chapter 14
Colleen

The scent of overheated chlorine assailed her nose as she stepped carefully on the tile surrounding the pool. She slung her towel on a rack, sliding her flip-flops underneath it, and eased into the water at the shallow end, gasping at the cold.

There were only a handful of swimmers, so Colleen was able to have an empty lane. She adjusted her goggles and pushed off from the wall swimming freestyle, kicking steadily. She swam several lengths before she stopped to catch her breath. The woman in the lane next to her approached the end, turned and continued swimming. Water dripped from the flesh hanging off her arms; her stroke was slow but determined. From the slack in her skin, she was in her 60s, maybe 70s.

Heartened, Colleen took a breath and pushed off again. That was the idea, wasn't it? That she'd be swimming steadily in her 70s? Forget how hard this felt and the fact that she hadn't swum in years. It would get easier. It had to get easier.

After a couple of weeks of self-medication attempts, she'd finally gone to her GP to figure out what was wrong with her back. He'd diagnosed her with a mild muscular strain and suggested not rest, but exercise.

"I run after three kids all day!" she'd said, the paper gown crinkling around her. "Isn't that exercise?"

Dr. Reynolds had folded his arms. "You don't have to tell me that. We have four kids and I *know* how much my wife does. But all that activity isn't enough. You need to strengthen your core, which includes your abdominal and back muscles. And it wouldn't hurt for you to get some regular cardiovascular exercise as well. Look at the pain you're having as a wake-up call to take better care of yourself."

"Isn't there anything else I can do?"

"Sure. You can keep taking analgesics, and the strain will eventually heal. But you're likely to experience the same condition in the future if you don't address the underlying muscular weakness." As if to underscore his point, her back had suddenly seized as she started to get up off the examining table.

The next day, she'd brought Jordan and the baby to the local Y. They'd been members for years, but she used the Y for the children's programs they offered. She hadn't even realized they offered free childcare until the early afternoon hours. She'd dropped them both off, stored her clothes in a locker, and taken a quick shower. Then she'd surprised herself by swimming for almost 40 minutes. Deduct the time she'd spent hanging on the edge of the pool and she'd still spent at least 20 minutes in motion.

The next morning, Colleen's arms and shoulders were stiff and sore, but she was surprised to find that her back actually felt better. Peter was standing at the sink pouring coffee into his travel cup when she came downstairs, rolling her shoulders in an attempt to work out the stiffness.

He screwed the top onto his cup and motioned for her to stand in front of him. She did, putting her hands on the sink, squinting at the early morning sun.

He squeezed the back of her neck, using both hands

to massage it before continuing down her shoulders and upper arms. "Sore?"

She groaned and Pete laughed. "Soreness is good, remember. It means your muscles are full of micro tears from being stressed. It's when those micro tears repair themselves that you get stronger."

"Thanks, doc."

He paused, and Colleen wiggled under his fingertips. "Don't stop!"

He turned his wrist to glance at his watch. "One more minute." Colleen turned her head from side to side as he palpated her neck up and down. "That feels better." She turned and kissed him. "Thank you."

"I'll do some more tonight if you're still stiff. Remind me," he added.

Colleen rolled her eyes, but smiled at him. The most frequent arguments centered around one basic concept: that she did more than he did. The corollary to that fact was that he never remembered to do what he'd offered to, or agreed to. She had to remind him, even nag him, the same way she'd remind Taylor that she couldn't wear her Irish step dancing shoes to school no matter how much she wanted to.

The mere fact that they even had arguments like this depressed her immeasurably. When they'd gotten married, and then when she'd been pregnant with Taylor, she'd promised herself she wouldn't fall into the trap she saw so many other married couples topple into. The man works. The woman stays home—and is responsible for the care, feeding, comfort, moral character, physical development, and life skills training of the children. She does the shopping, the cooking, pays the bills, wipes noses and talks to teachers and puts the kids in timeout and teaches them right from wrong and doesn't let them rot their brains staring at the television all afternoon and feeds them nutritious yet delicious food and makes sure that they feel special and secure and loved every minute. Dad? He shows up at the end of the day, tosses the kids around for fifteen minutes, making them squeal with laughter, and then is ready for them to go to bed. Except that then they're amped up and over-adrenalized, and won't sleep for at least an hour, and it's mom who will be coddling, wheedling, and finally threatening them into sleeping.

Colleen had been determined to avoid the clear imbalance in this kind of arrangement. After all, they were equal partners in the marriage. They could certainly play equal parenting roles as well.

But that is not what happened. Colleen wasn't sure what was worse. Having the lion's share of the responsibility for the kids and the house and everything that went along with it, or the fact that it had happened to her. She'd been smug. She'd thought, "That won't be *me*. Our marriage will be different."

Guess what? When it came to parenting, it was all but impossible to share the responsibilities equally. So why did that make her so angry?

It's because he gets a break, thought Colleen, making Taylor's lunch. He goes to work and can forget about all of us for eight, ten, twelve hours at a stretch. She was the one always on the hook to figure out what to make for dinner, to make sure Jordan had a gift for the birthday party on Saturday, to take the baby in for her next round of shots, to explain to Taylor that her gently curved tummy was not fat, no matter what that bony little mean-spirited Sasha had said and that she was not going to go on a diet at the age of seven. It was all up to her, unless Peter chipped in — and then she always had to remind him.

But there was no sense in complaining. This was how it was, and she'd agreed to this arrangement. And the kids were happy, for the most part, and on balance, that was worth it. Taylor sidled into the kitchen, still in her Hannah Montana pajamas. "Honey! You need to get going or you're going to be late for school."

Taylor reached past her to open the pantry, pulling out a box of Lucky Charms. "Mom! Hello! We don't have school today. Remember?"

Colleen stared at her for a second, then remembered. It was a teacher's institute day. "Oh, you're right." She put the half-made lunch back into the refrigerator. "Taylor, how about pancakes instead?"

"You don't usually make pancakes," said Taylor, her arms crossed.

"You don't usually have teacher institute days," said Colleen smoothly.

Taylor hesitated. "Can I help?"

"I was hoping you'd ask." She let Taylor mix the batter while she warmed the pan, and then showed her to drop just a dollop of batter onto the surface, and to wait until bubbles appeared on the surface to flip it.

"Perfect, honey." Colleen stood behind her daughter, tying an apron around her waist. Taylor painstakingly dropped equal-sized dollops on the griddle, her face serious, as Colleen watched. When had her chunky little toddler gotten so tall?

Jordan ran into the kitchen. "I want to help!" he said, running over to shove his sister. "And Rosie is crying," he said over his shoulder.

"Ow! Stop it! Mom!"

Colleen reached out and took Jordan's arm. "Leave your sister alone. She's the chef this morning."

Jordan pouted for a moment, but it was worth it to see the pleasure on her daughter's face. She brought Rose downstairs, and strapped her into her high chair. Taylor carefully scooped up several pancakes, and brought a plate to her little brother.

"Breakfast is served." Taylor set the plate in front of him, watching as he spread syrup on them. "I'm making yours next, okay, Mom? How many do you want?"

Colleen wasn't hungry. "How about three? I'll share them with baby Rose."

"They're delishus!" Jordan spoke with his mouth full of pancakes.

"They are, Taylor," agreed Colleen, as she sampled the pancakes. Taylor beamed.

"Did you notice how they're all exactly the same size?"

Colleen nodded. "And they're cooked just right. Not too runny and not too done."

Taylor made a plateful for herself, and Colleen reminded her to turn off the burner and turn the handle of the pan in. Rose was still too little to reach the stove, but it didn't hurt to teach safety lessons whenever she could. Taylor sat down, still wearing her apron and took a small, critical bite.

"I have to say they are quite excellent," she said.

"Maybe I should leave pancake-making up to you from now on," teased Colleen. "You could get up early every morning and make breakfast for us. What do you think?"

"No way! I'm just a kid!" But Taylor's face was pink with pleasure, and she put her dish in the sink without being reminded. Then she consented to play a game of Candyland with Jordan, without calling it a stupid baby game—and didn't complain when Jordan got the magic gumdrop card and crowed with delight. She looked over at Colleen and met her eyes.

"I loved to play this game when *I* was little, too, didn't I, Mom?"

Colleen laughed. "Yes, you did. When you were little. You know, before you knew how to make pancakes."

Taylor smiled, ducking her head, and hugged her knees to her chest before she reached for another color card. Colleen picked up the baby and pulled her onto her lap.

"Tell you what. When we finish this game, let's let Taylor pick one."

"But I don't know how to play all those games."

"I know." Colleen looked at her daughter. "How about if I help Jordan? That way the whole family can play."

Taylor considered, squeezing her legs to her chest, and nodded. "All right." She moved her game piece to a blue square. "Your turn, Jordy."

Colleen smiled at her daughter, feeling a rare sense of accomplishment. Her kids were clean, fed, and healthy, they were playing together, and miracle of miracles, they were treating each other with kindness. She thought of what Amelia had said, and decided to savor the moment. Which was fortunate, because that was about how long the perfect little family tableau lasted.

Chapter 15
Renee

Renee had been on her way out of work when Travis had taken her aside. She'd seen him come in and had nodded hello, but hadn't spoken with him. He followed her out of the store after stopping to help an older woman pull a cart free as she headed into the store.

"Renee, hang on for a second."

"Sure. What's up?" she said, zipping her coat.

"Nada. I wanted to say I didn't mean to chase you out of the store the other night," said Travis.

"What? Oh, that. It was no biggie. I had stuff to do," said Renee.

He nodded. "Understood. But I felt like you may have taken something wrong. Or rather, I said something wrong," Travis continued. "I wanted to remedy that if I did."

Renee didn't know what to say. "Well, thanks." She turned back to her car.

"We're good, then?"

"We're good." She'd been surprised at Travis' apology. Well, it hadn't been an apology per se, but it'd had the sound and feel of an apology, and she had accepted it as that. The flush of pleasure she'd felt at the fact that he'd made the effort, when he needn't, had confirmed for her at least that there was more than a friendly working relationship between them. And she was glad. Sure, she made chitchat and small talk with customers and coworkers alike, and spoke to Colleen every day or two, but the rest of the time away from work she could have been a monk. A silent one. Which left her feeling isolated—and lonely, she admitted to herself.

Sure, it was hard to believe that anyone could be lonely in a world of ubiquitous cell phones, but a cell phone that never rang only highlighted your essential isolation. That was why she thought so many people at the store were on their phones the whole time. They talked while they tossed bagged salad into their carts and studied the labels of frozen appetizers. They talked while they loaded wine and six-packs of beer and organic sugar-free apple juice into their carts. They talked while they stood in line, while their groceries were bagged, and they were still talking on their way out the door.

But Renee knew what they were doing—warding off loneliness. Too much time without the distraction of other people left you alone with yourself. Most people hated to be alone with their thoughts for even five minutes. Renee had never minded being alone, but she didn't want to live like a hermit for the rest of her life.

She'd stopped by the local library earlier that week to sign up for a library card, and fell into a conversation with the reference librarian, a woman in her early 30s. She had thick streaks of white blond in her dark hair, and fashionably skinny frames in her glasses. When Renee told her she looked too hip to be a librarian, she laughed aloud, then guiltily covered her mouth.

They had had a brief conversation, and Renee had come close to asking her out for lunch or coffee. But how to approach it? "Hi, I'm lonely. Will you be my friend?" seemed a bit abrupt, even scary. Besides, the woman probably had no room in her life for another person. It was only Renee who had too much space and not enough people to fill it.

She decided to make an effort. She'd take a class or join the Y...this was stupid. She didn't need to troll for possible friends. So there was an attraction between Travis and her. There was no reason to act on it. They could be friends. Why shouldn't they?

She debated how to bring it up, then decided to stop thinking about it. She wanted to go to the Art Institute, and the weather was definitely turning toward spring. If they had a matching day off next week, she'd ask him. If he said no, no biggie. He agreed. "Hey, I get to go with an expert guide, huh?"

"Actually I've never been." Renee pulled her coat on.

"You're kidding! But aren't you the art major?"

"An incomplete education, I suppose."

"We'll address that on Wednesday. I just need to get back for an afternoon workout with the team."

"Have you a plan?" Travis asked a few days later as they stood in line to buy tickets at the museum. "Or are we going to look at every piece of art in the whole place?"

But Renee had already considered that fact, and had in fact mapped out a basic strategy. "You said you don't care what you see, right?"

"Nope. I'm a veritable art virgin."

She made a face. "All right. We can't do justice to the collection in only a couple of hours, so I've chosen some works I've always wanted to see in person. You'll probably recognize some of them," she added, then cringed. He wasn't stupid, after all, but he didn't seem bothered.

He beckoned her past the steel-haired man taking tickets. "Lead on!"

They climbed the marble stairs to the second floor. "Here's what I was thinking. We could cover the impressionists and maybe see some Picasso, too."

"The French guys, right? Renoir, Monet, Manet?"

"Pretty good for a history major."

"Well, we did touch on France, you know."

"Heard of Seurat?" She gave it the French pronunciation, the emphasis on the second syllable rhyming with "owe" rather than "tot."

"Vaguely."

"He was an impressionist, too, but he's known for creating a style of painting called pointillism. He painted with little dabs of paint like dots. Hence the nickname Seurat the dot, if you take some license with your French."

He was walking next to her, hands clasped behind him. She stopped suddenly. "I'm sorry. I'm not trying to lecture you."

"No, keep it up! I'm interested."

They stepped into a large galley with a painting of a rainy city street displayed prominently in the middle. "Oh my gosh." Renee stared at it. "I didn't realize it was so huge."

Travis followed her. "This looks familiar to me." I haven't heard of the guy, though.

Renee checked the name template. "Gustave Caillebotte, *Paris Street: Rainy Day*." She stepped back from it to examine the overall effect. It was a large painting, carefully arranged in four quadrants. "See how the light post cuts the painting in half?" she said to Travis. "And the painting's bisected horizontally as well."

Travis leaned his head back, looking at it. "It does seem organized. All those straight lines."

They walked past the painting toward another, smaller one on the back wall of the gallery. The pretty feminine faces, the reds and blues and delicate paint strokes, were unmistakable. She looked at Travis.

"Renoir?"

"Very good!"

He tilted his head at the nameplate. "I cheated."

They walked slowly around the room, looking at the paintings. At one, *Woman at the Piano,* Renee stopped. "All right. Here's the thing with impressionists. They were obsessed with light and color—or more specifically, the way light affects color. See how her dress is mostly white, but with some blues, and grays as well? Then on her shoulder, there's some pink because that's the part of her body that's closest to the light source."

Travis stepped close to the painting. "Wow. You're right."

"How does it make you feel?"

"Seriously?" He studied it for a minute. "Relaxed. Or at least she feels relaxed. Peaceful."

Renee nodded. "Renoir was criticized by some of his peers because he insisted on painting happy, domestic scenes of beautiful people." She shrugged. "But some people only want to see something beautiful."

"Do you like him?"

"I like the impressionists, but I'd have to say Monet is my favorite." Renee was suddenly aware of how close Travis was standing. A couple in their 70s walked by, the woman's hand companionably on the man's arm.

"Why Monet?"

They walked into a room full of Monet paintings, and Renee gestured. "It's the brushstrokes, I suppose. He wasn't as concerned with simply duplicating what he saw, but using dabs and strokes of paint to suggest shapes. Look." She brought her face close to one of the paintings of a bridge. "See? You can even see the little clumps of paint that came from his brush."

Travis looked around the room. "He seems to be a bit obsessive, wasn't he? Looks like he had a thing for bridges," he said. "And haystacks," he added.

Renee smiled. "Actually he painted 100 versions of the Waterloo Bridge."

"What?" he leaned past her to read the wall. "Oh, you just read that off the card. Tell me something that isn't on here."

Renee thought. "Well, he loved to paint outside. You know all those haystack paintings? He'd take a stack of canvases and paint the same scene over and over as the light changed, trying to get the colors perfect."

"He must have spent a lot of money on art supplies."

Renee nodded as they continued walking. "He was broke most of his life, actually."

"The starving artist, personified."

"Exactly." That was the problem with art, thought Renee. If you were truly dedicated, you were expected to be broke as well—unless you found a wealthy patron or nowadays, a dealer and more importantly, a reputation and a well-heeled audience for your work. In some circles, even making it was considered selling out.

"What?" Travis caught her eye. "Thinking deep thoughts?"

Renee shrugged. "Just thinking about what a difficult life it must be." He didn't press and she didn't elaborate.

They continued walking, stopping occasionally to take in a particular painting. Travis didn't need to chatter, she noticed—he was quiet, watchful. It was almost like walking through the galleries alone—except that she was always aware of his presence. She was perfectly content, able to lose herself in the world of these paintings and yet know that she wasn't alone.

They entered another gallery and Renee smiled. "Wow. Come on," she said, ignoring the smaller works in the gallery. The painting, *Sunday on The Grande Jatte*, was the size of a small billboard and dominated the wall it was hung on.

Renee stood transfixed for a moment, feeling the

unique delight of experiencing a recognizable piece of art in person. How many times had she seen photographs of this painting, with its dozens of Parisian citizens taking in the air at a city park? But seeing it in the canvas, so to speak, was something different. She stood looking at it for several minutes, walking from one end of the room to the other while continuing to look at it.

"It's so much…more than what I thought. Wow."

Travis had been silent, waiting for her to speak.

"Tell me about it."

Renee smiled, shaking her head. "I had an art professor at Southern who was obsessed with Seurat, so I probably know more about that painting that any other." She walked to the right side of the painting, taking in the mix of bright and dark dots of color. "I can't believe how different it is to see it in person. It's hung wrong, though."

"What do you mean?"

She gestured at the man and woman in the front foreground of the painting's right side. "See how these two are larger than everyone else? Seurat meant the painting to be viewed from a 45 degree angle, not head on. Then the perspective works."

Travis nodded.

"There's some interesting social commentary in here too," said Renee. "See this woman fishing? She's thought to be a prostitute, and so is this woman in front with the monkey on a leash. Monkeys were popular pets among the wealthy at the time, but there's more to it than that. The monkey's an allusion to sex or lust, but it's on a leash, which makes it more genteel."

Travis nodded, and Renee started talking faster. "Seurat actually gives you lots of clues that this isn't supposed to be a representational painting—meaning it's not supposed to depict the scene as it appears. See? This tree has two shadows. Impossible. The smoke from this boat is blowing to the left, but the smoke from this boat is blowing to the right—which isn't likely. And if you look at these shadows toward the back of the painting? They don't match up to the trees at all. Seurat painted them to draw your eye back into the painting, but he also used geometric shapes in his work. The people in the painting may look randomly placed, but he was meticulous about choosing the pattern and layout of a painting as well as the colors he used."

She noticed a small group of people had gathered, listening with interest, and lowered her voice.

"Why are so many people shown in profile?" asked Travis.

Renee thought. "Seurat was studying Egyptian art at the time, which is known for profiles, and that influence is reflected here." She paused. "Actually he spent two years on this painting. He was so meticulous with his work that he was only able to finish seven large paintings during his career—and he died at the age of 31."

A well-dressed woman with long auburn hair spoke up. "Didn't Van Gogh die young, too?"

Renee nodded. "Yes, but he committed suicide. He struggled with depression most of his life and was institutionalized for a while."

"And he cut off his ear and sent it to a woman, didn't he?" asked the woman's companion.

Renee shook her head. "He did cut off his ear, but he didn't send it to anyone. I suppose it wound up on the floor of his studio."

A few people laughed, but the group remained standing there, hanging on her words.

"Can you tell me where I'd find Andrew Wyeth's work?" asked another woman dressed in a long blue coat.

"Ummm...I'm not sure. He's American, though, so his work wouldn't be in this gallery."

"Don't you work here?" said the woman, sounding affronted.

"No, sorry, I don't."

"She simply knows a lot about art," said Travis, smiling at her.

Renee answered a couple more questions, and the crowd started to drift away.

"Can I still walk with you?" asked Travis, teasing.

"Shut up." They continued walking, stopping briefly so Renee could consult the floor plan.

They reached the grand staircase and saw the pair of women from the other room. "That was fascinating," said one, waving at Renee. "Thank you for sharing all that!" Her companion nodded, and the two continued down the stairs.

Renee said nothing, and Travis gave her a gentle poke in the arm. "It was fascinating," he said.

"I didn't come off like a know-it-all?"

"You did sound like you knew it all! That's what made it so cool." He stopped to tie his shoe and looked up at her.

Renee didn't respond. Her mind was still crowded with thoughts of color and shading and paint dabs and dots of light and shadows and the wonder of translating life onto a piece of canvas. She had nearly forgotten how a selection of smears of colored oil could make you react, feel, question what was real and what wasn't. She had nearly forgotten how some works of art could transfix her, temporarily take her out of her everyday life, and imprint themselves in her brain forever. She had nearly forgotten, sure. But now she remembered.

Chapter 16
Colleen

Colleen waited for a VW bug to pull out ahead of her, waving her in. The woman, engaged in a conversation on her cell phone, skipped the customary thank-you wave.

Colleen slowed down for the light and waited for traffic to clear to turn left. Just as she started her turn, a minivan came racing toward her, intent on making the yellow light. Colleen slammed on the brakes, and the car shot past, the driver's cell phone held to her left ear. She accelerated to complete the turn and clear the intersection, pulling into the Blockbuster parking lot.

Her hands were shaking on the steering wheel. She whipped around to check the baby, who was clueless, a copy of *Shrek 2* in her mouth.

Colleen sat for several minutes, trying to calm her heart. Finally she climbed out of the car, dropped the movies in the slot ("You're on Time? You're so Kind!"), and got back in. Her arms and legs still felt wobbly, and her mouth tasted bad.

Rose complained from the backseat, and Colleen reached for her stuffed octopus, handing it to her. Immediately soothed, she cooed at the toy and grabbed it from Colleen's grasp. Colleen turned back and sat there without putting the car in drive. She could see Rose's chubby little arms waving in circles, the tentacles of the octopus dancing as she did so.

Colleen tried not to be one of those moms who was always dwelling on what could happen, but sometimes your mind just went there, all on its own. Her kids were healthy, sturdy, seemingly indestructible creatures. The idea that one of them might be hurt or taken from her was simply too enormous to fathom. You fed them healthy foods, carted them to the pediatrician for their immunizations, blocked the stairs, shoved plug protectors into every open socket, installed door locks on every low cabinet, snapped them into the car seat every single time, never left them in the bathtub unattended, chopped their food into miniscule bites when they finally began to feed themselves. You taught them about looking both ways and stranger danger and not to pet strange dogs and why it was a bad idea to shove pennies up their nose and took them (or rather, Jordan) to the emergency room when he went ahead and did it anyway and prayed that they would be safe. Then, blammo. A freak accident. One tiny cancer cell starts to grow. Your baby plays with the cord of the blinds when you're in the other room and it catches around her neck. Your son sees his dad behind the crossing gates and dashes in front of the train. Or one idiot driver, obliviously chattering away, slams broadside into your car and in an instant, all your worrying and seat-buckling and vaccines and nutritious foods cease to matter. Forever.

Colleen shook her head. She's fine. You're fine. You were paying attention. That's what's important.

She drove slowly to the Y to pick up Jordan, both hands on the steering wheel, eyes peeled to the rearview mirror. It wasn't until she retrieved Taylor from school and they were all home, Taylor and Jordan arguing over whose turn it was to play on the computer, that she relaxed. They were home. They were here. They were safe. At least for now.

That's something that Renee would never understand. No matter how deeply you loved someone—your mother, your lover, your spouse—it wasn't the kind of all-consuming, obsessive love you had for your children. Colleen remembered the horror she'd felt when Taylor, then three, had wanted to show her how big she was.

"Mommy, look! I can go down the stairs all by myself!"

Colleen had been carrying newborn Jordan downstairs, unaware that Taylor had awoken from her nap and trailed her out into the hallway. Colleen had turned to see her daughter sauntering down the center of the carpeted stairs. "Taylor! Hold the railing!"

Taylor's foot slipped, and she wobbled there for a moment. Then her momentum capitulated her forward and she bounced down the staircase like a stuffed animal. Colleen had nearly dropped Jordan in her hurry to get to her daughter. She laid him down, swaddled in his blanket, and grabbed for Taylor, who was amazingly still.

"Taylor! Taylor!" She scooped her up, forgetting that she might be making her injuries worse. "Oh, God! God, let her be okay! Please!" She was rocking back on her heels, Taylor's limp form in her arms.

Taylor coughed and began to howl. "Mommy! Mommy!"

Oh, thank you! Thank you! "Does it hurt? Show me where it hurts!" She pulled Taylor away so she could examine her body. Were her legs and arms still pointing in the right directions? Were there any bones jutting out of her perfect little limbs? Had she suffered a concussion?

"Come on, baby," she'd said, carrying her to the car. "We're going to the emergency room."

She'd strapped Taylor, still whimpering, into her car seat, grabbed Jordan, and sped to the emergency room, praying over and over that her daughter would be okay. By the time they'd arrived, Taylor was no longer crying, but insisted on Colleen holding her. She'd been rocking her, Jordan sleeping in his infant seat on the floor, when a young doctor with pockmarked skin had examined her and pronounced her fine.

"Kids fall all the time," he said, letting Taylor play with his stethoscope.

But he hadn't seen her cartwheeling down the stairs. "You're certain she's all right?" Colleen had stood there, tears of relief starting to form in her eyes.

"She might develop a few bruises or feel sore, but she's otherwise fine. No broken bones. No concussion." He'd bent down and lightly rapped on Taylor's skull. "You must have a pretty hard head there, blondie," he'd said and Taylor had giggled.

Colleen had let out a sigh, dropped her head and started to sob. She'd felt Taylor twist around in her arms.

"Mommy! Mommy, why are you crying?"

She'd lifted her head and pulled Taylor to her, kissing her chubby, soft cheek. "I'm happy. I'm just happy you're OK."

She still remembered the confusion on Taylor's face, her own cheeks still tear-stained. "You're crying because you're happy?"

Colleen had wiped her eyes and wrapped her arms around her daughter. "I am happy because you're not hurt. I don't want anything to ever happen to you, do you understand that? You promise me that you'll always hold the railing from now on. Promise?"

Taylor had nodded gravely, and Colleen had made eye contact with the young doctor as he stepped to the edge of the examining area. She mouthed "Thank you" and he smiled, nodding his head.

"Listen to your mommy. No more stairs unless you hold the railing!" He disappeared for a moment, and then returned with a sucker for Taylor. "For being a good girl."

"Taylor, what do you say?"

"Thank you," she'd said, reaching for the sucker. Whether it was her mother's reaction, the visit to the ER, or the terror of the day's events, the fall had made an impression. For weeks afterwards, she would only descend the stairs by gripping the railing with both hands, lowering each foot to the stair below as if dipping her toe into a hot bath. Every time Colleen saw her face tight with concentration, she'd had to press her lips together to keep from crying. But Taylor was OK—in fact, other than her meticulous stair climbing, she was unchanged, her fearless spirit intact. She didn't remember it happening. Colleen was the only one who still carried the terror of that moment, but most of the time she was able to keep it locked away deep inside. Except for sometimes, like today, when it escaped.

Renee would never understand any of this—not until she had a child of her own. Then again, look at Renee. The skin of her face might reveal that she was no longer in her 20s, but her compact body looked the same as it had when they were in college. Not to mention that she was free of the worries and obsessions that came along with parenthood. In that respect, Colleen felt a bond with the other mothers in the neighborhood—even those she didn't like—that was absent with Renee. Of course that woman in the minivan was presumably a parent too. Had her kids been in the car?

That night, Colleen sat down at the computer and fired off a letter to the editor of the paper. She recounted her near-accident and suggested that driving was an all-consuming responsibility. She even played the mom card. "As a parent, I take every precaution to keep my children safe. I'm sure the driver of the red minivan wouldn't knowingly endanger her kids or mine, but that's what she was doing when she was more focused on her phone conversation than the road. It's illegal to drink and drive," she wrote. "It should be illegal to dial and drive, too."

She emailed the letter, feeling a rare sense of satisfaction. At least she'd had her say.

Chapter 17
Renee

Spring was finally starting to let itself be known, in fits and starts. One sunny afternoon it reached the mid-50s; two days later, it snowed. Of course it was the slushy day that she wound up on cart duty, corralling the errant shopping carts from the parking lot. She gathered up twenty carts and replaced them in the front of the store. Coming in, she noticed that the front area of the store was wet and slippery from melted snow. She walked back to find a mop and bucket, and a couple of the yellow warning cones.

"What are you doing?" Pam stopped her, gesturing at the mop. "Aren't you supposed to be on cart duty?"

Pam had a way of doing that; asking questions she already knew the answers to. "I just finished," said Renee, her hands on the mop. "The front of the store is pretty wet, so I thought I'd mop it up."

Pam hesitated. "Oh. All right. Then give Zelieka a break on register three."

"Sure thing!" Renee sang. What was that woman's problem? Renee wasn't a teenager. She'd managed people before herself, and what she had normally would be considered showing initiative. But Pam's managerial style was not so much managing by walking around as it was giving people specific tasks that left no room for improvisation or creativity. Not that there was a lot of that anyway, unless you were charged with creating a new end cap display. Otherwise, you simply arranged the product in a neat, eye-catching manner.

But she hadn't minded about the lack of creativity before. At the mansion, she had been so busy putting out figurative fires that she hadn't cared whether she was using the creative side of her brain. Now that she had mastered most of the so-called skills of the job, she was starting to question how long she'd stay here.

She thought she'd come up with a solution, and pitched the idea to Travis one evening when the store was slow. She spoke to him while she restocked the paper bags under each of the registers.

"Hey, Travis, I know that Nancy is the regular sign person," she said between trips. She'd met Nancy a couple of times. She was an enormous woman with frizzy dark hair shot through with gray who wore overalls. Her fingers were always stained with chalk, and she hummed to herself as she worked. Renee had attempted to make conversation with her on several occasions, asking about her background in art, complimenting her on her designs, and the like. Nancy had been, if not downright unfriendly, noticeably disinterested in conversing with Renee.

"Anyway," she continued. "I was wondering whether the store would consider using another person for signs and stuff in addition to her."

Travis was standing at the computer at the manager's desk. He typed something in and then turned to look at her. "I'm sorry. What were you saying about Nancy?"

She slid a stack of bags under the slot of one of the registers and straightened up. "I wondered if she's all you need, or whether you'd ever consider using someone else. Even on a trial basis."

He thought for a moment. "I don't know the answer to that off the top of my head. Are we talking about you?"

She nodded. "I've got some ideas. They'd be different from what Nancy has been doing, though."

"Nothing wrong with different. What are you thinking?"

She turned away to greet a customer, quickly scanning her groceries and making small talk about the changeable weather. After the woman left, Renee glanced around the store, and then hurried over to the counter.

"I can explain it," she said slowly. "But I'd rather show you."

He shrugged. "You're the artist."

"Really?"

"Why not? Pam's the one with the final say on store signage but I don't see why not. Know where Nancy keeps her supplies in the back?"

Renee nodded quickly. "I do."

"There are extra chalkboards back there. Make a couple of signs and we'll take a look," said Travis.

"Great! I'm off at 8 tonight. Do you mind if I work on it after I punch out?"

He waved, preoccupied with the computer screen. "Have fun."

After Renee punched out and washed her hands, she carried a couple of chalkboards from the storeroom to the break room. She left Nancy's pail of chalk there; Renee had bought her own supply from an art store and brought it along with her. She tucked one leg underneath her, staring at the chalkboard. It was bigger than she had imagined—about four feet by six feet—and she needed to get her bearings before she drew the first few lines.

She hadn't worked with chalk before, save elementary school. The chalk was dusty, and the sides of her hands quickly became stained with a rainbow of colors.

But the idea of sketching was the same. She drew a couple of quick lines to break up the flat plane of the board, and then made light marks where she planned to draw various items. It was going to be a still life; a tabletop grouping of food and wine, with a purpose—all of the items were Dave's branded products. After she had confirmed the placement of the objects, she stood up to begin actually drawing each one, careful not to smudge her work. As she worked, she lost track of herself, focusing only on using the limited number of colors she had to make the objects look real rather than primary-hued cartoons.

"Cool." Dylan was standing at her shoulder, and Renee started. "Sorry. Didn't mean to freak you."

Renee straightened up, putting the piece of chalk down and flexing her fingers. She checked her watch. "It's 10:00 already?"

"Yeah. I'm outta here." He grabbed a dingy gray sweatshirt from the coat rack, which stunk of cigarette smoke. "Later."

"Is Travis still up front?"

"Yeah, but he's closing up. Better jet unless you want to be locked inside all night."

"Thanks." Renee carried the chalkboard back to the storeroom, careful not to smudge her work, and stowed it facing the wall. Nancy had been here this week, so it was safe to assume that she wouldn't return for a few more weeks—she appeared once a month or so to create new signs.

She grabbed her coat, and hurried up to the front. Travis was shutting down, turning off the store lights. "Didn't even know you were still here," he said.

"I got caught up in what I was doing."

"The artist at work." He checked the computer screen and stepped out from behind the counter. "Is your work ready for an audience?"

"Not yet." She smiled. "You'll be the first to see it."

"Good enough." He followed her outside. "You heading home?"

"Uh huh. Unless...I don't know. You want to get a drink someplace?" Renee was careful to keep her voice neutral, friendly.

He jingled his keys. "Why not. O'Malley's?" He named a nearby bar she had driven by before.

"Meet you there." Renee started her car and sat there for a moment. The fingers of her right hand were stiff and could still smell the chalk in her nostrils, but her body felt light. Instead of feeling tired, her mind was already planning the next board. She'd do another still life, but this one would be outside. A picnic scene, maybe.

She hurried inside the bar. Travis raised his hand at her. Three different televisions above the bar showed three different shows—two basketball games and a Cheers rerun, quite apropos. Travis was sitting at a small round table, and Renee joined him, shrugging off her coat.

"I'm going to wash my hands," she said, holding them up. "Back in a second."

"I'll get our drinks. What do you want?"

Renee considered. "A glass of wine. Pinot grigio." That was what Colleen always had on hand.

"Coming right up."

In the wood-paneled bathroom, she washed her hands, looking at her reflection in the mirror. Her cheeks were pink, and her eyes looked happy. She grinned at herself.

"Thanks." There was no waitress, and Travis had brought the drinks back to their table. She took a tiny sip of wine.

"You're a wine drinker?"

"On occasion." Mollie had not only introduced her to the intricacies of wine tasting but to foods she would have never tried before. She didn't believe you could suggest a particular bottle of wine or house brand liquor or oysters Rockefeller to a client unless you had tried it yourself. Renee grimaced, recalling the slippery feel and briny taste of an oyster sliding down her throat.

"What? Don't like it?"

"No." She took another small sip. "I was thinking of oysters." She explained, and Travis nodded.

"So this isn't the first job where you've been a paid taster."

"Exactly."

He took a long drink. "Do you miss it?"

"I miss the people I worked with. I miss Mollie—she's the woman who owns the mansion," said Renee, taking another small sip. "I don't miss the drama and the last-minute crises and servers not showing up and country club ladies who want everything just so…"

He interrupted. "country club ladies?"

"You know. Ladies who lunch. They don't have to work, so they throw themselves into golf and tennis and throwing parties and of course, some kind of charitable work to make themselves feel better about being so well-off," said Renee.

"Maybe they truly care about making the world a better place."

"That's possible. Regardless, down to a woman, they're high-maintenance with a capital H," said Renee. "Everything must be perfect." She shook her head. "I had to carry my cell phone all the time, and always be available and understanding and efficient and gracious." She took another sip of wine. "That wears on you after a while."

"Mollie's your old boyfriend's mom, then?"

He'd remembered. "Yes, she's Lars' mom. Though she felt like mine too."

"So, what happened? With Lars?"

"Do you really want to know?" she asked, stalling.

"Why else would I ask?"

"Polite conversation?" asked Renee.

"I get paid to have polite conversations, remember?" said Travis. "I try to avoid those in my off hours."

"That's...that's a wise philosophy," said Renee thoughtfully. "But what does that leave?"

"Meaningful conversations. Not the kind of small talk that greases the social wheel. So?"

"It's an old story. Boy meets girl, boy gets girl, boy decides he doesn't want girl," she said, keeping her voice even. "Not that it was that simple." She took another sip of wine, noticing that Travis had already drained his glass. "The bottom line is that I wanted more than he did. I wanted to get married. He didn't."

"That's a problem," he said. "So where are you now?"

She knew he meant emotionally, not geographically. "I'm...I'm good. Not completely healed, but there's no more gaping wound. So that's progress," she said.

"Good to know. You seem happier than you did when you started at the store."

"I do?" But she was happy at work, she reasoned. It was only when she was alone that she still felt adrift. "I don't know that I'm happier. But I'm more whole," she said slowly. Does that make sense?" Suddenly she realized that her loneliness might mean something positive—that she was *aware* of space in her life that needed filling. Space that she wanted to fill.

He indicated her drink. "You want another?"

She eyed the glass, which was half-full. "No, I'm fine."

He came back with a fresh drink and two glasses of ice water.

She gestured at his glass. "What are you drinking?"

"OJ."

"OJ and..."

"Just OJ."

"Oh."

He took a gulp of his juice. "I don't drink."

"Oh." She sat there for a moment. "Because you're the coach for the college kids?"

He laughed. "No, although I suppose it doesn't hurt to set a good example. No, I quit a couple of years ago."

"I am so sorry! I should have never asked you to come to a bar!" She felt huge, ridiculous, stupid.

"If I couldn't handle being in a bar, I would have said no," he said. "Besides, this isn't exactly my first time in one since I quit."

"Oh, all right." Renee still felt stupid. "Why didn't you tell me?"

He shrugged. "I figured you knew. It's not exactly a secret." He looked amused.

"Why did you quit?" Renee had a sudden flash of her mom, and of the countless people she'd seen at the mansion who had been what mansion employees called "over-served." She'd known plenty of people who should have stopped drinking, or at least drastically cut down on what they consumed. Her mom came to mind. She hadn't met anyone who had actually done it.

"It was a crutch for me," said Travis. "And when it got to the point where I couldn't function without it, I got worried."

"Did you...hit bottom?"

"I don't know. What's hitting bottom? Getting a DUI? Winding up in jail? Losing your job?" He leaned back from the table, crossing his arms over his chest. "I don't think you have to bottom out to quit. I think you decide that something isn't working any longer. And you make a change."

Renee thought about leaving Lars. Leaving St. Louis. Leaving everything except Colleen. "I'm familiar with that concept, actually."

166

He nodded. "I thought you might be. I admire your willingness to take that kind of risk. Most people wouldn't." He raised his orange juice glass. "To someone I admire."

She clinked her wine glass against his, wondering if she had alcohol on her breath, and sat there looking at him. Renee could hear the over-excited basketball announcer babbling in the background, and felt the slightly stiff leather of the bar seat against her back. Her body felt both lax and yet hyper-aware of everything happening. She could imagine sliding off of her seat into a puddle on the floor, or leaping up to perform any physical task necessary. Anything was possible.

Finally Renee spoke. "I don't live very far from here," she said. "Would you like to see my apartment? Maybe have some more, um, juice?" She nodded at his empty glass.

His smile was slow, and genuine, and sexy. Extremely sexy. She hadn't noticed that before.

"Absolutely. I'll follow you there."

They both stood up, pulling on their coats, and Travis carried their glasses up to the bar. She smiled inwardly. Women often bussed their own tables at a bar, but rarely did a man show that kind of thoughtfulness. She took that as a good sign.

Chapter 18
Colleen

"Come on, Taylor!" Colleen shouted. "It's time to go home."

Taylor scowled, and crossed her arms over her chest. Her hair had been pulled up into a topknot, and she wore a tiara glittering with fake diamonds and other jewels. Her eyes were elaborately made up, with sky blue shadow and lashes that were thick with mascara. Round splotches of blush and red lipstick gave her the appearance of a child prostitute.

Colleen had her doubts about the "princess party" theme, but the birthday celebration of Sasha was the event of the seven-year-old season. It had been held at an upscale shop called "Little Darlings," which featured dress-up parties for little girls. Like the other girls, Taylor had changed back into her street clothes, but she refused to remove the tiara.

"No, Mom!" she said, when Colleen reached to take it out of her hair. "I get to keep it."

Colleen looked over Taylor at the woman who owned the shop. She was even more heavily made up, wearing an encrusted tiara of her own and a chiffon dress of ruffles that floated around her like an elaborate wedding cake. "That's right. The tiaras are for the little princesses to take home. So they always remember that there's a little princess in each one of them."

Colleen pictured Taylor punching her younger brother in the arm for refusing to change the channel. Not quite the behavior of up-and-coming royalty, but she had the imperious nature down pat. "Let's get going, honey."

Taylor complied, chattering about the party as she climbed into the backseat. "Sasha said she liked my gift better than anyone else's. She said that the doll Mackenzie gave her was stupid and just for babies!"

Colleen looked at her daughter in the mirror. "What's wrong with giving Sasha a doll?"

"Mom. It wasn't even a Bratz doll. It was a stupid baby doll. Sasha said it was the *worst* present she ever got. In her whole entire life."

Colleen sighed. When would Taylor find a new best friend? "That wasn't very nice. What did Mackenzie do?"

"She cried." Taylor's voice was matter-of-fact.

Colleen looked at Taylor in the rear view mirror. "How would you feel if it had been you who got her the baby doll?"

"But I didn't! I got her the exact American Girl outfit she asked for! Mackenzie was the one who got her the stupid baby doll."

"Maybe Mackenzie thought the doll was a good gift. But that doesn't matter. It was rude of Sasha to say she didn't like what she got. And it was really mean to say it in front of her. Do you see that?"

Taylor's hand twisted up into her hair, turning a curl around her finger. When she was a baby, she'd done the same thing; shoved one thumb in her mouth while playing with her hair with the other hand. "I guess."

"You guess? How do you think Mackenzie felt when Sasha said her gift was stupid?"

"Bad." Taylor's voice was small.

Colleen pulled into their driveway, depressing the

button for the garage. She turned off the engine and turned to face her daughter. "That's right. Because you know it doesn't feel good when someone's mean to you. Especially a friend."

"I know." Taylor unbuckled her seatbelt and then looked up at her. "I know, Mom!"

Colleen shook her head. The kid wasn't even eight years old. What would happen when she hit puberty? She followed her into the house.

"Why don't you show your dad your tiara?"

"Yeah!" Taylor pounded down the hall. "Dad! Dad, I got to be a princess!"

Colleen heard Pete's voice. "You did? Jesus, what's that on your face?"

Colleen came in, setting her purse on the kitchen. "That's her princess look, honey." They exchanged a glance over their daughter's head.

"I see." He bent down to investigate her tiara more closely. "This looks like it might be valuable. Maybe we can hock this for your college fund."

"Da-ad," said Taylor. "It's pretend diamonds, not the real thing." She leaned up against him as he straightened up, affectionate as she rarely was with Colleen.

He snapped his fingers. "Too bad. Thought we had it made there." Peter looked at his watch. "We have plans tonight?"

"Nothing special."

He bent down suddenly, snatching Taylor up. "What do you say you and your brother and I go play some basketball at the Y? Or are you getting too old to do that?"

Taylor squealed. "Yeah!"

He spun her around for a minute while Colleen watched. It was so easy for him. She was trying to teach morals, sensitivity, and life lessons and he was teaching them how to nail a jump shot. Then again, she'd never been good at sports.

"Jordan!" Colleen called. "Your dad wants to know if you want to play basketball!"

She heard Jordan's whoop from upstairs, then the sound of him galloping down the stairs. "I want to go!" He came skidding to a halt in front of his sister. "What happened to your face?"

Colleen and Pete tried not to laugh. "I'm a princess, stupid."

"Taylor..."

"Hmmmm. You know, I don't know if princesses play basketball," said Pete thoughtfully.

"Dad! They do too. Princesses can do anything they want. Look at Princess Jasmine."

"Still, how 'bout you wash your face before we go?" Taylor considered.

"Of course the Y closes pretty soon..."

Taylor interrupted him. "Just a minute!" She dashed off to the bathroom.

"That was pretty slick," said Colleen to Peter. "Jordan, go get your shoes on."

"OK, Mommy." He hurried off.

"I've still got some tricks," said Pete. "Besides, I don't want to show up with our little Pretty Baby in tow."

"Isn't that awful? I don't know what her mother was thinking. You should have seen all the little girls leaving the party. They looked like a pack of Jon-Benets."

"That's a scary thought." Peter picked up his car keys. "Where's my basketball team?"

"Coming!" Taylor appeared, her face damp but still smeared with makeup.

"Coming!" echoed Jordan.

Colleen dampened a paper towel, stepping over to her daughter to remove the rest of the mascara and blush. Taylor frowned as Colleen finished.

"Hey! There's my beautiful little girl!" Peter picked her up, swinging Jordan under his other arm. "I barely recognized you under all that makeup."

"Dad! I'm not a little girl anymore!" But she squealed and laughed, throwing her head over his shoulder.

"We'll be back in a while."

Colleen pointed upstairs. "Is the baby napping?"

"Yup. She went down a while ago. You want me to pick anything up on the way home?"

Colleen considered. "Pizza?"

"Pizza! Pizza, pizza, pizza!" yelled Taylor.

"Pizza! Pep-roni!" echoed Jordan.

"Pizza sounds good." She gave the three of them a quick kiss. "Have fun!"

Colleen glanced around the kitchen. Pete had made lunch for Jordan and the baby while she was gone. A crumb-covered plate sat on the counter next to an opened bag of nacho chips, and the baby's highchair tray was covered with globs of orange-colored food. Colleen dampened a sponge and cleaned up, then walked upstairs to check on Rose.

Rose was lying on her stomach, hands tucked under her legs. Colleen pulled the blanket up over her back and stood looking at her for a moment. Rose was losing that infant fuzziness as she moved into toddler-hood. Her arms and legs were sturdy, like her older siblings, and the two little teeth jutting out of her bottom gum was a further reminder that soon she'd give up the bottle entirely in favor of solid food.

Would they still call her the baby even as she outgrew her baby status? She was still her baby, after all. At least for a few more months.

Colleen returned to the kitchen, then dug out her trusty stack of magazines and curled up on the couch. She had an hour, maybe longer, to herself—an opportunity to do anything she liked. So why was she using this precious, finite time to flip through trashy magazines? She already knew Brittney was pregnant again, that Tom Cruise was still dragging the enormously pregnant, lank-haired Katie Holmes around by the hand, that Brangelina, while a couple, had not actually tied the knot yet. She'd read so many of these magazines there was nothing actually new in them.

Colleen sat there for a minute or two, staring at the stack. She tried to count how many minutes she'd wasted losing herself in celebrities' lives and couldn't. She'd justified buying them by telling herself she'd needed an escape, an interlude from her real life. But once she shut the magazine, there was her real life, waiting for her. No amount of distraction was going to make it just go away, and it certainly wasn't helping her feel any less overwhelmed or any less lonely. Suddenly she stood and swept the entire stack into the garbage, surprised at the loud thud they made as they hit the bottom of the can.

Chapter 19
Renee

Renee came back to awareness, lying on her back. Her eyes were closed, but she couldn't help smiling. Months of no sex had made her almost forget how all-encompassing good lovemaking could be, how you could lose yourself, even lose track of time, lose track of everything, at least for a few minutes.

"Hey."

"Hey." She rolled over to face him.

"You okay?"

She nodded. "Oh, I'm okay. Better than okay."

"I don't want to assume..." he started. "In the interest of customer service, may I ask if you're satisfied with your recent sexual experience?"

She laughed. "Yes. This customer is satisfied." She looked at him, but his face was serious. "Really. That was amazing. Couldn't you tell?"

She saw his face relax. "Yeah, I thought so. But I wanted to be sure."

Renee couldn't help being touched by his concern. He was so confident, so easy in his own skin, that she forgot he would have had the usual worries and hang-ups any guy had when it came to sex.

"Relax," she said, leaning forward to kiss him. "I

will say it's been a while," Renee admitted. "I think you figured that, though."

"For me, too."

That was good to know. He didn't seem like the kind of guy who would jump into bed with just anyone. At the same time, she didn't want to hash over details or even gross generalities of their past relationships. And she certainly didn't want to talk about Lars, though she couldn't help but make comparisons between the two at this exact moment. "Renee? I'm glad you invited me here," he said.

"I am too." She hesitated. "But I don't know that I'm in the right space to start something new. Can't we just be—I don't know, something else? Friends hanging out together?"

"Oh, right. The old 'friends with benefits.'" He tucked his hands behind his head, giving her a chance to admire his body. He was thinner than she had thought, with no visible fat on his body. His skin was stretched tight, and his smooth chest was pale compared to his arms, which still showed a faint farmer's tan.

"I don't have to put a name on this," he said finally. "If you want to, that's your call."

Renee sighed. Sleeping with him had probably been a mistake. Sure, it had seemed right, a lethal combination of loneliness and attraction and opportunity propelling her into bed. She'd been thinking that maybe they could kiss, touch a little, hold each other. "Make out" like she used to in college.

But she had underestimated her desire—and maybe his, too. Their kissing had quickly led to groping, panting, and more kissing. Tongues, tongues, and more tongues. He had stopped once, his breathing loud, to say, "You want this?" and Renee had grunted yes, struggling to pull his jeans to the floor. There was the strangeness of his body—so compact, so skinny compared to Lars—and the unfamiliarity of the way he kissed, the way he'd moved inside her. Now she was naked in bed with a guy she worked with. Hell, a guy she worked for! Yes, she liked him, but hadn't she learned anything from her former life?

"You regretting this?" Travis' voice jolted her back.

"I don't know," she lied. "Look. I like you. I'm obviously attracted to you. Beyond that, I don't know. Is that fair?"

"Fair enough." He leaned over to kiss her. "Let's drop the subject. The world is full of things we can talk about. Music. Art. Philosophy. Favorite foods. Places you've been. Places you want to go. Pick a subject, any subject. Sound good?"

"Conversation and companionship, that's what's on the agenda?"

"Yeah, though I have to say it's a bonus to be doing it naked in bed." He rearranged the pillow so he was sitting up, his back against the wall. "You never did tell me about your sign inspiration. What's up with that?"

Renee tried not to smile. He wanted to know. "Just a minute." She scrabbled on the floor for her underwear and a shirt, pulling them on before she stood up. "I'll be right back."

She pulled a couple of bottles of water and a package of oatmeal raisin cookies out of the miniscule kitchen cabinet and brought them back to the bed. She'd forgotten about the outdoor still life since they'd left the bar, but he'd been paying enough attention to remember. And he'd brought it up. They talked for a while, and Renee felt her body sliding into that relaxed pre-sleep stage. She yawned.

"I'm going to get going," he said. "I've got to open in the morning."

She was relieved, but surprised. Not that she wanted him to spend the night. Or did she? He kissed her briefly. "I'll lock the door," he said. "Get some sleep."

Renee didn't work until noon the next day. When she punched in, Travis was at the manager's desk, talking to Pam. He nodded at her, and she waved at him. She could have sworn that Pam frowned at her, but she was always frowning about something. "Renee, you're on the floor," said Pam. "Make sure you check and clean the bathrooms on the hour."

"No problem, Pam," sang Renee. She found herself humming under her breath, flashes of the night before interrupting her thoughts. She did like him. There was nothing wrong with that. So what if they worked together? She knew it was never a good idea to get involved with someone you worked with, not that that fact stopped anyone from doing it. Of course, as her boss it technically was *his* responsibility not to get involved with her.

Renee thought back to the Dave's employee manual. Was there a policy against employee fraternization? She couldn't remember. But she certainly wasn't going to announce that they'd slept together to the store as a whole.

After her six-hour shift, Renee walked over to the nearby Panera to kill time until she saw Pam leave the store.

"Back so soon?" Travis was back at the desk, working another split shift.

She indicated the back room. "I thought I'd do some work, if that's all right with you."

"Enjoy."

Renee found the chalkboards and sat down to finish the first one. It hadn't turned out exactly as she'd imagined, but she liked the way the colors contrasted.

She sat down to sketch out the next one and had a sudden flash. She wanted to do a picnic scene, so why not an homage to *Dejeuner sur L'Herbe*, or "Luncheon in the Grass?" Manet's painting had scandalized the public when it was first displayed, and most people would recognize it today — if only because it featured a naked woman flanked by two fully dressed men. The way she looked directly at the viewer was unsettling; yet the woman appeared completely at ease. There was no undercurrent or worry of suggested rape; rather, the three appeared to be good friends enjoying a picnic. Renee sketched the scene from memory, with the idea of placing a few Dave's products where the fruit, mussels, and bread would have been.

She used a larger-size chalkboard for this drawing, but it worked, giving her room to duplicate the layout and draw recognizable products. Over the upper right side, she added a few taglines. "Picnicking in the Grass? Don't forget crunchy French loaf, bruschetta, and Dealin' Dave's delicious Brie—and a bottle of our Oregonian chardonnay."

Renee considered her work, propping it against the wall. It didn't have the depth that the original had, but then again she wasn't painting with oil. With only a handful of colors of chalk, she thought she'd done a decent job.

"Wow."

Travis had crept up behind her, and she jumped. She stepped in front of the chalkboard. "Wait! I'm not ready for anyone to see it."

"Come on." He placed his hands on her arms, gently moving her out of the way. " That's amazing. He noticed the Dave's products and started laughing. "Renee! That is great! I've never seen anything like this before." He bent down to look more closely at the chalkboard. "This rocks. We've got to use this."

"You're not just saying this?"

"Hell, no." He squeezed her shoulder. "I think we should hang this above dairy where everyone will see it. Plus you've got a naked woman on there. That's bound to command attention."

Renee flushed, delighted. "Still, though, do you think Pam will go for it?"

"Why not?"

Renee rubbed her hands together, noticing how filthy they were from the chalk. "Let me do a couple more. Then I'll be ready to show them to her." She went to pick up the chalkboard and Travis automatically went to grab the other end.

Renee paused at the door to the back room where she'd been working. "You working late tonight?"

He grinned. "No, but I've got an early morning practice with the team, so I need to catch some sleep. I didn't get much last night."

"Oh, okay. I'll see you tomorrow, then." She walked out, surprised that he hadn't offered to come over. And, she had to admit, disappointed too.

Chapter 20
Colleen

By the time she finished the laundry, Peter was in bed, reading a copy of *Sports Illustrated*. Colleen climbed under the covers, tucking her body around him.

He automatically shifted his body and put his arm around her shoulders. She lay there for a moment, looking at his profile. He had a few more grays at his temples, and his forehead had grown a bit higher, but otherwise he looked like the same 25-year-old she'd fallen in love with.

"What are you reading?"

"Predictions for the year's baseball season." He turned a page. "We're what—not even two months in? But this could be the year the Cubs go all the way."

She slid her hand under the waistband of the baggy cotton shorts he liked to sleep in. "You say that every year."

He made a noncommittal noise and Colleen slid her hand lower, into the curly hair at the base of his pelvis. He didn't say anything but she felt an almost imperceptible thrust upward toward her hand.

"Don't do that unless you mean it."

"Hmmm?" She continued to touch him. He put down the magazine.

"Lady, what are you doing to me?"

"Come on, it hasn't been that long. You must remember."

He pulled her underneath him, sliding his hand up the side of her body. "Vaguely. Why don't you remind me."

"Turn off the light," Colleen murmured. "I'll remind you."

And she did. Their lovemaking had lost the edge of passionate desperation it had early on, but it wasn't the kind of sex Colleen was often guilty of—when she only initiated sex out of a sense of obligation or duty. If you wanted to be a good wife—and if you wanted a happy husband—having sex when you didn't particularly feel like it was the price you paid. If you wanted a delighted husband, you even initiated it.

But this wasn't that kind of sex. She'd been looking at him at dinner, the five of them sitting at the table eating pizza they'd had delivered. He had told the kids the story about when she'd taught him to drive a stick shift shortly after they'd started dating.

"You didn't know how to drive a car?" Taylor had looked skeptical at the idea that her beloved daddy couldn't master every task.

"Not a manual," Peter had said, giving Taylor another piece of pepperoni. "Our cars are automatics, which means the engine shifts the gears for you. In a manual car, you do it yourself."

"And you couldn't do it? But Mommy could?"

"Yup." He grinned at Colleen. "And she said she'd show me."

"So what happened?" Taylor had asked.

"It was like this." He pantomimed a car jerking back and forth, adding automotive screeching noises. "And your mom laughed her head off."

"You did?" Taylor gave an accusing look.

"I did." Colleen started to laugh, remembering how

sweaty and frustrated Pete had gotten. She'd kept telling him to let the clutch out easy, but he lacked finesse and kept stalling the car. She'd tried not to laugh, but a giggle had snuck out.

"It's not funny!" He'd said, which had only made her laugh harder. "Holy shit! What the hell is wrong with this car?" he'd yelled in frustration.

"Oh, it's the car! Not the driver," she'd laughed, and he'd looked over at her and finally seen the humor in it.

"It looks easier than it is," he'd said in an attempt to save face. He wasn't angry anymore, preferring to laugh at himself.

"I learned to drive a manual when I was fifteen," she'd added. "Which makes it easier than learning as an adult."

He'd looked at her and suddenly kissed her. "What else can you do that I can't?"

She'd smiled, stroking his face. "You'll have to find that out, won't you?"

"Oh, I'm going to do that," he'd said, giving her a look that had left her feeling weak. "You can bet on it."

Tonight she'd remembered that, and recalled the way they were as a couple, before the kids came along. The sex had had the sense of emotional connection that wasn't always there now. "What got into you?" he said sleepily. "And how do I make it happen again?"

She kissed his chest in the dark, not wanting to explain. Pete sighed, and his breathing started to deepen. She didn't mind. Her body felt loose and warm, and she drifted off to sleep without realizing it.

The next morning Colleen awoke with a start. What sound had stirred her sleep? She sat up in bed, straining to hear, and then stole down the hallway to check the kids' rooms. The baby was asleep on her stomach, her hands tucked on her body. Taylor was sleeping starfish-style and Jordan was curled like a cashew under his blanket. It was close to 7 and they were all three still asleep.

Colleen crawled back into bed. Peter stirred. "The kids are all still out. You mind if I go for a walk?"

He mumbled something, and Colleen stole outside, careful to ease the door shut behind her. The air was chilly, but the sun felt warm on her face. She took a minute to stretch, and then set off at a relaxed pace. Within a few minutes, her breath was coming faster, and she unzipped her jacket.

She couldn't remember the last time she'd been outside this early, alone. Dew hung on the grass, the air smelled sweet, and so far the streets were quiet without the usual weekend morning sounds of lawnmowers and kids. She thought of Pete, of her kids all cozy and asleep (quiet for once) in their beds and felt a sudden rush of gratitude. Why did she only seem to appreciate what she had when she was away from it?

By the time she got home, Peter was up with the kids. He'd fed them cereal and Taylor and Jordan were sitting with glazed eyes in front of a morning cartoon. The baby was in her high chair, gnawing on a teething biscuit, globs of which were stuck to her face.

"Hi." She kissed him, and he grabbed her around the waist.

"I had a hot dream last night," he murmured so the kids wouldn't hear.

She wrapped her arms around him and gave him a real kiss. "How strange. I did, too." They stayed like that a moment, until Taylor's attention was momentarily diverted from the television.

"Gross! Do you have to do that in front us?"

"What's that?" said Peter, peppering her face with little pecks. "I can't hear you. I'm busy kissing your mother."

Taylor stood up, crossing her arms over her chest. "Dad, you are dis-gusting sometimes." She drew the word out for emphasis. Jordan got up, trailing after his sister, afraid he'd be left out of something important. Colleen told him to turn off the television.

"It's going to be nice today," she said. "Let's do something as a family."

"Chuck E. Cheese's!" yelled Jordan, throwing his fist in the air.

"That's for babies." Taylor crossed her arms again, scowling.

Colleen rolled her eyes. "I seem to recall that last time we went, you were the one who had to be dragged out kicking and screaming."

"I did not." But she uncrossed her arms and bent down to get the baby's sippy cup Rose had thrown without being asked.

Colleen looked at her husband. She should have run this by him before springing it on the kids, but he wouldn't mind. Besides, all he had to do was start the car. She had to gather up juice boxes and snacks and diapers and wipes and bottles and jackets and the baby's stroller, shepherd each child to the car and make sure that they were all dressed appropriately. Jordan would wear shorts and his team tank top during the dead of winter if she let him.

"How about...the zoo?" She looked at Pete. He nodded.

"Sounds good. As long as we get to see the monkeys."

"Dad! You always want to see the monkeys."

"Why is that?" He pretended to think a moment, then suddenly grabbed Taylor around her middle, lifting her off the ground. "Could it be that my kids are monkeys too?"

Taylor squealed and Jordan jumped in, throwing his arms around his father. He lifted him off his feet, too, and glanced at Colleen. "Maybe we'll leave you both at the zoo!"

The kids screamed and laughed, and Colleen wiped the baby's face, letting her crawl over to join the pandemonium. "Honey, here comes the baby."

"I got her." He lifted her carefully as she chortled, pinning the other two kids, one under each foot. "What do you say, babe? Should we drop them off at the zoo?"

"We'll see. Maybe they're looking for a few more to add to their collection." It took another hour to get out the door, and they spent the better part of the day at the zoo, and then stopped for ice cream as a treat. By the time they got home that night, Rose was sound asleep and Taylor and Jordan were cranky and tired. Overtired, over-stimulated, and over-sugared with giant cinnamon rolls. They were all in bed, with no complaints, by a little after 7 that night.

Peter slid open the door to the porch, where Colleen was sitting, her feet propped on a deck chair. He had a Sam Adams in his hand. "You want a glass of wine?"

"No, I'm fine."

Pete checked the grill, poking the steaks before he closed the lid. "A few more minutes." He leaned against the railing, looking at the yard. "See those yellow patches? We've got grubs." He gestured with his beer bottle.

"Which means?"

"Means I'll have to spray the lawn."

She took a sip of her water, enjoying the dying spring sunshine and the sounds of birds, insects, and the noise of families making the most of their Sunday evenings. "Will that be okay for the kids?"

"I'll read the label. Relax."

She closed her eyes, leaning her head back. "Remember when we spent every summer Sunday like this? Sitting outside on that tiny deck in our place in Lakeview?"

"I remember." He came to sit beside her, pushing the chair so they could both put their feet up. "PK." He grinned. "Remember what I said about having kids? 'How much work can a baby be?'"

"I remember." She poked his leg with his foot. "Spoken like a true youngest child." Colleen had been six when her brother had been born. He always had been screaming about something. He needed a bottle. He needed a clean diaper. He needed to be held. That's what her mother had said, anyway, but Colleen had promised herself she'd never have one of those red-faced, smelly, loud little things. Especially after her second brother had arrived eleven months later.

But of course she had. When she fell in love with Peter, she'd realized for the first time how powerful the desire to procreate could be. It wasn't just that she wanted a baby. It was the all-consuming feeling of wanting to create a person that had sprung from their love. She'd been thrilled to get pregnant immediately, with no clue of what awaited her on the other side.

Colleen returned to the kitchen to make plates for both of them, roasted potatoes she'd tossed in the oven, and hot corn from a saucepan on the stove. He served their steaks and they ate in silence. Colleen savored the food, the wine, the sound of the breeze in the trees, and was content.

"These are great, honey," she said, chewing a bite of meat. "Thanks for cooking."

He nodded, intent on his food.

"Pete?" She set down her fork and took a breath. "How would you feel if I said I wanted to go back to work?"

He looked up, surprised. "What? We're fine on what I make, aren't we?"

She sighed. "It's not that. The money is only part of it. I miss being someone more than Taylor's mom or Jordan's carpool driver."

"We both know that you're more than that."

"That's hard to remember most days." She leaned

forward and took his hand. "Look, I know what we've got. I appreciate how hard you work so I can stay home. But what if I looked for something part-time? That could work, couldn't it?"

"Colleen, think about it. If I'm on the road or working late and you're at work, who's going to take care of the kids?"

"Because that's my job, is that what you're saying?"

"It's both of our jobs. But it was your idea to stay home," he said in a reasonable tone—the one he used when he was just waiting for her to discover that he was right. "And we agreed that it was the right thing to do."

"We agreed. Past tense. Now I'm saying things have changed. I want to discuss it."

He finished his dinner and set his silverware on his plate. "There's nothing to discuss, is there? Unless I quit work and become a stay-at-home dad, and that's not going to happen." He saw her face and softened. "Come on, babe. None of your friends work, do they? We're lucky that you don't have to."

Colleen nodded, her hands in her lap, and let it drop. She wasn't even sure that she wanted to work, or that she could figure out a way to fit any kind of job into her life. But she wanted to talk about it, hash over the pros and cons, discuss it with the person in her life whose opinion mattered the most. The fact that he dismissed her so readily made her feel guilty for even considering it. Especially considering how lucky she was.

Chapter 21
Renee

The thing about grieving is that you never quite know when you're done. Renee had thought she was finished. She was wrong.

Lars had called her the week before, to remind her about Christina's graduation party in early May. She'd received an invitation from Lissa the week before but hadn't answered.

"Look, Renee, I don't know what to tell you. Everybody misses you. My mom would love it if you'd come, and Christina and Lissa would too."

She didn't say anything. "I'll think about it."

"You can't even say yes? You know Christina loves you." He lowered his voice. "Look, I promised my mom I'd get you here. You don't want to make a liar out of me, do you?"

"No." Renee bit her lip. She had to go back sometime. It wasn't as if the part of the country west of the Mississippi had slid into the ocean. Maybe this was her opportunity to close the door on this chapter of her life, and move on to the next, whatever that was going to be.

She wasn't sure what to say to Travis about it, so she said nothing. Someone else's heartbreak was never as interesting or as compelling as your own, after all.

Either way, though, she'd have to ask for the weekend off to make the party. It shouldn't be an issue—Renee had worked every Saturday and Sunday since she started four months ago. The next afternoon, Renee found Pam at the manager's desk.

"Pam, do you have a second?"

Pam looked up. Hostility radiated off her like heat off summer asphalt.

Pam didn't say anything, just looked at her expectantly.

"I need next Saturday and Sunday off. I'll be out of town."

Pam said nothing, but pursed her lips.

Renee mentally rolled her eyes. "I have worked every weekend since I started here. Taking one off isn't a problem, is it?"

Deep sigh from Pam. Renee waited. She'd dealt with bosses like her before in high school and college. It didn't matter how many legitimate, compelling reasons you had for taking time off. In the service industry, you were expected to work every weekend and just about every holiday as well and to prostate yourself and beg like a homeless person for a day off. Renee waited her out.

"I suppose I'll have to make it work." Pam frowned, apparently reorganizing next weekend's schedule in her mind, which involved planning along the lines of Napoleon's invasion of Russia.

"Super. That's great. Thank you so much." Renee drenched her words with as much heartfelt sincerity as she could manage.

If she had to beg for this, how was she going to get Pam to consider using her store signs? Travis had offered to speak to Pam for her, to "soften her up."

"What are you going to do, tenderize her with a wooden steak mallet?" asked Renee. "Not that I would mind."

They were sitting on her couch, legs entangled, eating popcorn and paying half-hearted attention to a *South Park* rerun. Travis gravitated toward juvenile comedy, which no doubt made him popular with the college kids he coached. She'd attended one of the meets on a Saturday morning, watching an assortment of skinny, sinewy, single-minded kids tearing around the indoor track. It had taken her a while to spot Travis — he was wearing the college colors and blended in with the rest of the team.

"No, don't say anything."

"Come on. Think of me as your patron." He ate a handful of popcorn. "I can not only vouch for your talent, but I can help you get your first commission."

"You think Dealin' Dave's would pay me to do the boards?"

"Why not? They pay Nancy, don't they?"

Renee rearranged her legs, tucking her feet under Travis's butt. "It's her job to make signs. I'm only a lowly 'associate,' remember?"

"You won't know unless you ask."

"But *I* should ask. Even thought she doesn't like me."

Travis didn't say anything.

"Travis, I mean it."

"What's the big deal? Why can't I help you if I want to? I know Pam better than you do."

Something in his voice caught her attention. "What does that mean?"

"I've worked with her for three years. I know how she works. She's not comfortable with authority, so she tends to overuse hers."

"I'm aware of that," said Renee. "And she doesn't like me."

Travis rubbed his face for a minute. "Yeah, well, she asked me if we were 'seeing' each other," he said.

"What? Why would she ask that? Have you slept with anyone else at the store?" Renee pulled away from him.

"Just one person," said Travis.

"What? You have? Who?" She stared at him. "You slept with *Pam*?"

"Yeah, we have some history together," said Travis.

"History?" she prompted.

"We had a thing a couple of years ago," said Travis.

Renee's mouth hung open. "A thing. With Pam. Who hates me," she said. "And now I know why. So did you tell her we're...seeing each other?"

"I'm not going to lie about you," he said.

Renee crossed her arms over her chest. "Why out of all people, would you sleep with Pam?" Yes, she was beautiful. And she had a great body, Renee could see that. She glanced down at her own less-than-abundant breasts. But was Travis that...shallow?

"I have asked myself that question more than once. What can I say? Britta and I had broken up, I made some bad decisions. Though screwing my boss was probably at the top of the heap."

Renee stayed where she was. "Were you still drinking?"

He laughed. "Hey, I can't blame alcohol for every bad decision. Though the first time, yeah, I was pretty lit."

"There was more than one time?"

"We dated for a while. A month or two. She went a little whacko on me."

"How so?"

"She got clingy. Wanted every second of my time. Started talking about us leaving Dave's, opening our own business together. She had our life mapped out based on some so-so sex." He laughed. "Which was my fault. It's hard to be good in bed when you're trying to pretend your partner is someone else."

191

Renee flushed. Did he think *she* was good in bed? She liked sex with him, she knew that. She liked the way he kissed. She liked the way he paid attention to the way she responded. His body had felt strange to her after years with Lars, who was larger, broader, and less graceful, but that in itself was exciting. She hadn't realized how lazy you got when you'd been with someone for so long until she'd had sex with Travis and had to worry about her performance. Presumably he liked what she was doing—after all, he was here, wasn't he? But then again, he'd slept with Pam. With Pam!

He was watching her. "Renee. This isn't a big deal. Don't make it into one."

She half-laughed. "At least now I know why you said they never enforce the no-fraternization policy." She sighed. "I just can't believe you didn't say anything to me." She experienced a feeling she hadn't had with him before. Was it loss? Was it doubt? That was it. She'd felt a connection with him, a sense of possibility. Now that possibility had been tainted with mistrust.

Chapter 22
Colleen

Colleen hit "send," and pushed back the chair from the computer. Pete was lounging on the couch, watching Sports Center.

"Get your rant out?"

"I did." He moved to make room for her on the couch without being asked.

"Feel better?"

She shrugged. "I suppose." She stretched, yawning. "Venting is tiring business."

"You think they'll print it?"

"I hope so." To her surprise, the local paper had printed her anti-cell phone letter. Even more surprising, people had read it—several of her neighbors had commented on it. One woman, a parent at Taylor's school, even said she'd started keeping her cell phone in her purse because of her letter.

After that, Colleen had written several more letters. One about smokers who threw their cigarette butts out their car windows—after she found a bunch of cigarette butts in her front yard. One about parents at kids' athletic competitions who took the games way too seriously after a particularly aggressive father at one of Taylor's soccer games had screamed so loudly the referees had asked him to leave the field. "What was wrong with that man, Mom?" Taylor had asked, her eyes wide.

You can't tell your seven-year-old some people, some parents even, are assholes. "He must have really wanted his team to win."

"But it's not about who wins," Taylor had parroted. "It's about playing as a team and having fun."

Colleen didn't point out that the last time Taylor's team had lost, she'd sulked the rest of the day. "That's exactly right, honey." She'd sat down that night at the computer, pointing out that it was hard for kids to learn good sportsmanship when their own parents had no manners, let alone restraint.

"You might think that you're encouraging your children with your showoff enthusiasm. Maybe you even think you're helping win the game. You're not. You're embarrassing them, you're scaring them, and you're humiliating them—not to mention yourself. Head to a professional sports arena if you want to rant and rave. Those adults are paid to listen to jerks in the stands and bleachers. But in the meantime, *stop screaming at my kids*."

Writing the letters gave her a sense of pleasure. She didn't miss reading her celebrity mags, choosing instead to find things "to rant about," according to Pete. But the letters had freed her in some way. The next time a smoker flicked her butt out the car window at a stoplight, Colleen didn't grab the steering wheel and seethe. She smiled and shook her head. Each letter was like a valve that released some of the pressure that seemed to always be building up. She even surprised herself by writing a positive letter—an anti-rant, if you will—about the generosity of her neighbors when they raised money for victims of Hurricane Katrina.

But she was still shocked when the phone rang a few days later.

"Can I speak with Colleen Driscoll?"

Another phone solicitor. What a great way to start the day. "Speaking," said Colleen.

"This is Michael Walensky. I'm the editor of *The Daily Tribune*."

Colleen nearly dropped the phone. She'd sent one too many ranting letters—now her name was probably on a list somewhere. "Uh huh?"

"You are the Colleen Driscoll that has written letters to the editor, correct?"

"Yes." Colleen shut the water off and dried her hands on a towel. "Why? Have I reached my limit?"

"What? No!" He laughed. "I hope not, anyway. I don't know if you saw, but we're adding a couple of new features to the paper. Want to give it a stronger local feel, set it apart from the city papers. The only way to compete is to focus on the local."

So why was he telling her this? "Uh huh," she said again. Great. He probably thought she was a typical brain-dead housewife.

"We're going to try something new—local columnists' takes on living in this area, juggling busy lives, that kind of thing. We want to hear from a 'typical' resident and we think you'd be great. You want to give it a shot?"

"You mean I'd write, like, a regular column?"

"Yeah. The columns would be longer than typical letters to the editor. I'd need 600 to 700 words once a week. We'd pay $35. We'd need three to get started, then we'd want you to do one every week afterwards."

"I don't know...what if I run out of things to write about?" said Colleen, thinking out loud.

"I can send some ideas your way, or you can cover stuff that's happening here in the community. You've got carte blanche topic-wise as long as there's some kind of local tie-in."

"Wow." Colleen sat down at the kitchen table. "I

thought you were calling to tell me to stop writing letters to the editor."

"No, we love your letters. They're smart and topical and most important, opinionated. That's why we thought of you."

"I'm flattered," she said. "Um, sure. I'd love to. When would you need the columns by?" They agreed to a date two weeks away, and she hung up the phone before quacking dialing Pete's office number.

"Guess what? The local paper just offered me a weekly column."

"You're joking."

"I'm not! I couldn't believe it!"

"You're going to turn it down, aren't you?"

"Why should I?" Colleen frowned.

"Writing letters is one thing," Pete said. "But when will you find time to write a weekly column?"

"This is different," said Colleen. "This is something I want to do." And she did. The editor didn't care that she was a mom or a wife. He only cared that she wrote smart, opinionated letters. It's all about me, she though with glee. For a change.

"If you're sure you can handle it..."

"I'm sure, all right? Now why don't you congratulate me."

Peter got the message. "That's great, honey. Congratulations."

"More," she said.

"Congratulations!" he said, with much more enthusiasm. "I'm sure you'll do a fantastic job."

"Keep going..."

"What? What am I forgetting?"

Colleen waited, smiling.

"Oh, yeah. I love you. And I'm proud of you," he added. This is why we're still married, she thought as she hung up the phone.

Colleen invited Renee over for a celebratory dinner the next night. The kids were in bed, and Peter was working late.

Renee hugged her when Colleen shared her news. "Colleen! That is so cool!" She raised her glass of wine. "A toast to you! Wow, to think I'm friends with the local columnist! I can't wait to read your first column!"

This was what Colleen had wanted — pure unadulterated excitement with no pointing out of potential drawbacks. She smiled a huge smile. "Thanks. I'm excited about it. I've already got a list of topics and have started on my first couple of columns."

"Tell me when the first one runs so I can brag about you at the store." She sipped her wine. "Oh, this is good. This is the first drink I've had in weeks, do you realize that?"

"You're kidding." How many nights had Colleen downed a big goblet of wine? Too many to count, Colleen realized, and decided not to share that. She was drinking less now though and that's what was important.

Renee shrugged. "Travis doesn't drink. He says he doesn't care if I do, but I can't imagine he likes kissing me with booze on my breath." She took another sip. "I figure it's like kissing a smoker when you've quit, you know?"

Colleen spread some cheese on a baguette and handed it to Renee. "Does he do AA or anything?"

"Nope. He says he doesn't agree with the victim mentality. Says for him, at least, it's a matter of deciding not to drink — instead of working the steps or whatever it is they do." Renee shrugged, tucking her hair behind ear. "I can tell you after years of working around people who shouldn't be drinking, I don't mind it at all."

"Are you and he — getting serious?" Colleen rolled her eyes. "That sounds ridiculous when you're in your 30s, doesn't it?"

"I don't know what we're getting. The sex is — it's

great, actually. I'm still annoyed about the whole Pam thing, but I can't help what he did before I came along, can I?" said Renee. "I just like him. I like talking to him. I like being around him. I think of him as a friend. And more," she admitted.

"You're not over Lars." It was a statement, not a question.

"I don't know. Do you ever really get over someone?" Renee looked at her plate. "The thing is, I still love him. I don't know if that will ever go away." She sighed. "But that love isn't doing anything for me, you know? So I'm going to try to focus on what I loved about him, and what I learned from him, and move on." She made a face. "Don't I sound mature?"

"Amazingly mature. You know, Amelia says people come into our lives to teach us lessons we need to learn."

"Is she your friend who teaches yoga?"

Colleen nodded, loving that phrase. "Your friend who teaches yoga." Because she and Amelia were friends, or at least on their way to becoming same.

"Oh, great. So what lesson am I supposed to be learning from Pam?"

"I don't know. Humility? Patience?" Colleen laughed. "I'm only a writer. I don't claim to have all the answers."

"Do you think dating Travis is a mistake?" Renee asked suddenly.

"I don't know, Renee. I think you seem happy, though, and that's the most important thing."

Renee smiled. "I am happy. Or at least happier than I was. I'm starting to realize that even though I loved Lars, I put stuff on hold for him. I don't want to do that anymore. I don't want my whole life to be tied up in one person. Does that make sense?"

"Yeah, but it's kind of impossible when you're married and have kids. Everything flows from that."

"I hadn't thought of that. But Pete made a commitment to you. You guys made a conscious decision to be together. I think Lars never made a decision like that. He just kept going in the direction he was already going, and I went along for the ride. I'm not going to do that again."

"That sounds smart."

Renee was quiet for a moment. "Colleen, can I ask you something? Have you been upset with me? You always seem so busy every time I call. I thought maybe… you thought I was horning in on you and your family."

"You'd never be horning in." Colleen felt a sudden flash of guilt. It wasn't Renee's fault Colleen had been unhappy. "Can I be brutal?"

Renee nodded. "I'm ready."

Colleen took a deep breath, trying to find the right words. "Sometimes I feel like you belittle me."

"What?" Renee's face was shocked. "How so?"

Colleen forced herself to keep going. "You act like my life is small and typical and meaningless. And boring! 'Don't you get bored at home all day?' You remember asking me that?"

"Uh—no, not specifically."

"Well, I do get bored. And frustrated. And overwhelmed. But it's one thing for *me* to say I get bored. It's something else when your best friend implies you couldn't be anything *but* bored." She tried to keep her voice even. "That's a pretty clear condemnation of my choices, isn't it?"

Renee opened her mouth and closed it. "It wasn't a condemnation at all. That isn't how I meant it," said Renee.

Neither said anything for a minute. "I didn't realize you were so angry," said Renee.

Colleen sat down and took a quick sip of wine. "I didn't either. I'm sorry."

"Sorry for what? You can't apologize for telling the

truth, remember? Not when I asked for it." Renee sighed. "I've been wrapped up in my own life. And you seem so sure of everything. It didn't occur to me that you were unhappy. *Are* you unhappy?"

Colleen could feel her sudden anger fading. "Sometimes. I don't know. I feel bored with my life sometimes. Then I feel guilty for being bored, when I have what a lot of women would kill for." She laughed, feeling her body loosen a bit. "Which is probably why it made me so mad when you asked about it. Boredom and guilt are a powerful combination."

Renee looked at her, her face serious. "Want to talk about it?"

"Yeah, I do." Colleen crossed her legs. "Just not right this minute."

The two of them sat for a moment, and then Renee reached her hand over. Colleen took it.

"Are we still best friends?" Renee said in a small voice, playing but still serious.

Colleen nodded. "Are you kidding? Of course."

Renee squeezed her hand.

"But let's be *better* friends."

Renee nodded. "Exactly."

Chapter 23
Renee

She pulled up a half-block from Lissa's house, a classic colonial on a cul-de-sac, and sat there with the engine idling. There were balloons dancing in the warm, humid air in front of the house, and cars parked along both sides of the street. Renee recognized Lars' black Explorer and Kathy's red BMW.

It was near to 5 p.m., so the party had been in full swing for a while. She stepped out of the car, a present for Christina under her arm, and locked the car behind her.

She walked with her head high, in case someone was peeking out the windows. Act happy. This is ridiculous, she thought. I *am* happy. I'm fine. My life is going great. I'm just here to see people I care about. No biggie.

She rang the bell, and the door was opened by Genevieve, Christine's younger sister by five years. She was wearing a yellow dress with an enormous bow on the back, and her normally messy hair hung sleek under a matching yellow headband. But her knees, Renee could see, were skinned and bruised.

Genevieve goggled at her for a second. Then she shouted "Renee!" and threw her arms around her before suddenly pushing her away.

"Where have you been? You missed all my volleyball games!" She crossed her arms over her chest, her eyes narrowed.

"That's a long story, Gen." Renee followed her into the noisy house. The front hall was decorated with pink and purple balloons—Christina's favorite colors—and a pair of four-year-olds darted past them. "I'll tell you later."

"All right." Another child, a boy close to Gen's age, dashed out and pulled on the ribbon on her dress.

"You're going to get it!" She pounded after him, and Renee followed the noise into the huge great room. There were about 30 people in the room, a mix of adults and kids from Christine's age down to a tiny baby riding in a sling on her mother's chest. Renee waved at Lissa, who deep in conversation with another woman, and Christina, dressed in a pink sweater with appliquéd flowers and a straight pink skirt. She had the small, high breasts and the long coltish legs of youth, and burst into a braces-bared grin when she saw her.

"You came!" Christine hugged her, eying the gift. "And you brought me something!"

Christine reached for it and shook it experimentally. "It's not very heavy. Is it something good?"

Renee had been stumped, and had ended up buying a gift certificate from Old Navy. "Tell you what. I promise you'll like it."

Christine tossed the package onto the table behind her, then caught Renee's eye. "Oh no! It's not breakable, is it?"

"I hope not," said Renee, and then shook her head.

"Gram, look who's here!"

"I see her." Renee turned to see Mollie standing next to her. Her short hair was streaked with blond, and in her slim-fitting sea-foam suit, she could easily pass for her mid-40s. "Hi, sweetheart." She put her arms around Renee and gave her a long hug.

It wasn't the physical contact that undid her. It was Mollie's familiar smell, a floral perfume Renee had forgotten until now. Her eyes filled with tears, and when Mollie pulled away, Renee saw her eyes were wet too.

"It's good to see you."

Renee nodded, smiling and wiping at her eyes. "You too."

Mollie put her arm around her. "Come on, let's get away from all these people." She led her out to the backyard. Yellow daffodils and red tulips were poking out of the beds next to the cedar deck.

"So, how are you? Are you all right?"

Renee nodded, unable to speak. Mollie waited.

"I'm sorry," said Renee finally. "I'm sorry I left like that."

"I told you before, you don't have to apologize." She waved her hand. "That son of mine. I thought Lars would come around eventually, marry you, and give me a few more grandkids."

"Me too." Renee forced a smile. "I guess he didn't get the memo."

Mollie nodded. "Daughters are so much easier. Sons, you never know what's going on in their heads."

Renee nodded, resisting the urge to commiserate about Lars. Mollie might be her friend, but she was still his mother, after all.

Mollie dug into her little clutch and pulled out her cigarettes. "Have to smoke outside anyway, away from the grandkids. Genevieve keeps drawing me pictures of black lungs and telling me that's what mine look like." She lit and took a long drag, blowing the smoke away from Renee. "Tell me how you are."

Renee had recovered her composure, and crossed her arms over her chest. "I'm good. I'm working at a Dealin' Dave's, and I've got a cute little apartment," said Renee. "And you remember Colleen. I see her and her family a lot."

"What about your love life? Are you seeing anyone?"

Renee hesitated. Then again, did it matter? "There is someone..." she said finally.

"Oh, thank God. I'm so glad. I hate to think of you wasting the best years of your life on him," said Mollie, one hand on the deck railing. "Not that it's any of my business."

Renee didn't know how to respond to that. Was she supposed to agree that the six years in love with her son were a poor way to have spent her time? She had the sudden urge to flee. What had she been thinking? She had appreciated Mollie's directness before. Now her blunt talk felt like a weapon.

"How's work?" said Renee, sidestepping. "Are you busy with graduation parties?"

Mollie finished her cigarette, grinding the butt with the bottom of her shoe, then picking it up and wrapping it into a tissue, which she put in her purse. "I hired a new manager—her name is Jodi. She's taken up the slack and then some."

"Oh. That's good." So Renee had been easy to replace. She cast about for another conversational topic. Before she and Mollie had spent hours talking—about what? About work. Planning menus, commiserating about difficult clients, gossiping about movies or Mollie's husband, daughters, and grandkids—or just as likely, Lars. Renee had felt as close to her as her own mother—closer, in a way. Now she felt like distant relations, with some blood in common but nothing else.

"Did you see him?" Mollie nodded her head at the house.

"No, not yet."

Mollie didn't say anything, just reached out and squeezed her arm. "Who knows. Maybe he'll realize what a fool he's been when he sees you."

They returned inside, and Renee saw Lars by the fireplace, Genevieve hanging onto his arm. He was wearing a dark blue and brown striped shirt and chocolate brown cords. She'd bought him those pants, she remembered.

He looked up and saw her, and bent down to say something to Gen. Renee waited for him to reach her.

"You came."

"You guilted me into it."

They stood there awkwardly, and then he reached out to embrace her. "Hi."

She felt his familiar solidity and warmth and realized she'd made a mistake coming here. She wasn't ready for this.

She pulled away, not meeting his eyes. "Do you think I could get a drink?"

"Yeah, sure." He steered her toward the kitchen. "Water? Wine? What would you like?"

"Water's fine." He poured himself a glass of something red and drank some, watching her. "Strange, huh?"

She nodded. She'd thought she'd severed the connection between the two of them, but something—some strings as thin as gossamer, impossible to see—still hung there. The room was noisy but she was conscious of little but how close he was standing to her.

"Let's go outside." Lars indicated the sliding glass door she and Mollie had just returned from. She followed him outside, both relieved to escape the mass of humanity that was Lars' extended family (how had she forgotten how many people they were related to?) and dreading having to be alone with him. "Come on. This is strange enough. Let's not add my family on top of it." They escaped back outside without anyone noticing.

"So." Renee was back on the deck, this time with

Lars. She tucked her hair behind her ear, wishing she was at Dealin' Dave's, restocking wine, or rounding up the scattered carts in the parking lot, or loading cardboard into the crusher. Anywhere but here. She'd told herself she was coming for Christina. But she'd really come here for him. She'd wanted to see him, and now that she had, she regretted making the trip.

They talked for a while, but later Renee wouldn't be able to remember what he'd said, or what she'd said. She'd been thinking this is it. This is the last time. The last time I'll stand this close to him. The last time I'll smell him. The last time I'll touch him. Then, the last time I hug him. The last time I feel him kiss me goodbye.

Renee tried to take mental snapshots of the way he leaned his body against the railing, the clean smell of his Cool Water cologne, the timbre of his laugh. These would be things she would want to remember. She'd put these things away for now, and one day she'd be ready. She'd be able to take these pictures out of the box and look at them more closely, without it hurting so much.

Chapter 24
Colleen

By the time Colleen finished cleaning up the kitchen after dinner, Peter had rounded up the kids and sent them upstairs to get their pajamas on. They came trampling down the stairs, and Colleen grimaced.

"Daddy! I found the story for you to read us!" Jordan held up his copy of *Where the Wild Things Are*. Ever since he'd overcome his fear of the enormous-toothed monsters in the book, it had been his favorite.

Taylor followed close on his heels, carrying a *Babysitter's Club* book in her hand. Sasha had two older sisters and Taylor had to read everything she did. "Dad, no! I don't want to read a baby book."

Peter looked at Colleen, his hands raised. "What do you think? Divide and conquer?"

Colleen dried her hands on the towel. "Sure." She picked Taylor's book. "Haven't you read this one?"

"No, Mom." Taylor's tone was aggrieved. "This is a new one. There's a whole series, you know."

"Pardon me for not knowing." She put her hand on Taylor's back. "Come on, we'll read in your room."

Taylor stopped. "I thought Dad was going to read to me."

Peter had hoisted Jordan up over his shoulder and

was carrying him up the stairs. "Come on, sport."

"Dad! I want you to read to me."

He turned on the stairs and saw Colleen's face. "We'll trade off, kiddo. I'll read to you tomorrow night."

Taylor stuck her lip out and folded her arms across her chest. "You said you were going to read to us! Not just Jordan!"

"Geez, the kid's a lawyer in the making." He looked at Colleen for help, but she simply waited to see what he'd do.

"Hey, sport, how 'bout if Mommy reads to you tonight, and I read to you tomorrow night?"

He should have known that delayed gratification is a weak motivator for most adults, let alone a not-quite-five-year-old. Jordan's lip quivered. "Noooo! You said!"

Colleen leaned against the banister, torn between amusement and hurt. They always wanted Daddy. Mom was only good for feeding you and getting you dressed and getting you to school on time and kissing scraped knees and taking you to birthday parties and making the classes' special snack and reminding you to wear your Brownie uniform on Thursdays. Daddy was all about wrestling matches and trips to McDonald's and playing ball in the backyard and the kind of roughhousing where something inevitably got broken.

It was Melissa, surprisingly enough, who had pointed out why Daddy stock always outranked Mommy's. "They're a rare commodity," she'd said. "Moms are always available, so there's less demand for them. If you only see your daddy for less than an hour a day, who are you going to want?"

Though she hated to admit that Melissa could ever be right about anything, it made sense. It was easier to be a good dad than a mom, easier still if you had limited time with your children.

Come home, throw them up in the air, make them

laugh, and you qualified for Daddy of the Year. Moms not only were held to a higher standard, but had a more demanding job as well—especially when they stayed home.

This fact seemed so obvious to Colleen now. Her job as a parent was always going to be more difficult than Pete's unless they switched roles, and she didn't see that happening. She stood in the hallway and listened to him attempt to cajole both kids. He finally resolved the standoff by agreeing to read *Wild Things* first, then a chapter from Taylor's babysitting book. She smiled. She'd known he'd cave, but it was nice to know that they weren't any easier to please—at least with some things—with him than they were with her.

Pete reappeared a half-hour later, dropping on the couch next to her. She was sitting with a notebook, jotting down some ideas for future columns.

"Whatcha doing?"

"Working on some column ideas."

"Oh yeah?" He picked up the remote. "Mind if I turn the tube on?"

She didn't answer, watching him as he flipped to a recap of the White Sox game. "What if I say yes?"

"Huh?"

"What if I say yes, I mind if you turn the TV on?"

"What? What." He muted the volume. "If you don't want me to watch TV, I'll go upstairs."

"That's not it. I don't mind. It'd just be nice if you waited for an answer before you went ahead and did it." Like you do just about every night, she thought to herself but didn't add.

He eyed her for a moment. "I can do that."

"That's it." She smiled and leaned over to kiss him. "Thank you."

"You sure that's it? You don't want to tell me how I never listen, and how not listening is the first symptom of a marriage breaking down, and how I take you for granted..." His voice was even, but she could hear an undertone of anger.

Colleen held up her hand. "Nope. That's it."

He looked suspicious.

Colleen set down her pen. "You know, I've been working on these columns and I've been thinking. I started out with these rants but that's not enough if I'm going to do a weekly column. I want to write about other things."

"Yeah, like what?"

Colleen hesitated. "Like how hard it is to have a good marriage. How easy it is to take your spouse for granted."

"Again, I'm supposed to be paying attention right about now, right?"

Colleen reached over and touched his arm. "Honey, look. I'm talking about myself, not just you. I'm tired of feeling angry or resentful or unappreciated or overwhelmed," she said. "But you can't help if I don't tell you I need help."

Colleen waited. When you marry someone, you take a huge risk. You're betting that this person won't simply promise to stand by you in good times and bad—that he will actually do it. You're betting that he'll be the husband, the partner, the parent you've convinced yourself he will be. And of course you're also betting, or at least hoping, that the two of you will remain in love, and that the inevitable disappointments he causes you will only be insignificant ones. That when it's time to step up to the proverbial plate, he'll come out swinging.

Sometimes those kinds of long shots pay off. Pete snapped off the television, turned to face her, and said, "So tell me, hon. Tell me how I can help."

**Chapter 25
Renee**

After she punched out, Renee washed her hands and slipped off her Dave's vest, the official sign that she was no longer in helpful-to-every-customer associate mode. She walked to the stockroom, humming under her breath. The store was featuring inexpensive wine from an Oregon winery—merlot, cabernet, chardonnay, and sauvignon blanc. Renee had been unloading wine boxes when she'd had a sudden flash—a symmetrical four-framed drawing with a bottle of wine in each one. She'd had Andy Warhol on the brain lately, having just seen some of his work at a traveling show, and the resulting work would be familiar enough for most people to "get it."

"Oh, hi, Nancy."

Nancy was sitting at the long table in the back, bent over a chalkboard.

She barely looked up, mumbling hello.

"Working on some new signs?" Renee scanned the room. There were a few chalkboards leaning against the wall in the corner. Those must be hers.

"Looks like."

Renee ignored the hostility. "Do you work in other media? Besides the work you do here at the store?"

Nancy lifted her head, her lips pursed with

concentration. "I do some painting. Watercolors, primarily. I've been working on a series of Chicago cityscapes, atmospheric stuff."

"That's great. Watercolor is a difficult medium."

Nancy checked her face for signs of sarcasm or contempt and apparently found none. "I suppose."

Renee leaned on the table, wondering how she could check on her own chalkboards without Nancy noticing. Doing her own Warhol-inspired sign was out of the question while she was sitting here.

"I've shown a couple of times, never solo though." Nancy finished outlining some bright green jungle leaves and set her piece of chalk down. "Why so interested?"

"I'm interested in art," said Renee. That much was true. "Actually, I have a little bit of a background in it, but more nontraditional stuff."

She briefly described her card business and Nancy listened, her sign forgotten. "There's a market for that kitschy stuff, especially now. I bet you could get your stuff into some of the independent bookstores, those kinds of places. A friend of mine makes jewelry—unique, gorgeous stuff—and she's got eight or ten stores that sell it for her. Plus she sells stuff through her website."

Renee thought of the boxes at home, stored on the floor of her closet. She hadn't opened them since she'd moved up here. Then again, why had she bothered to bring them with her? "I could never make a living at it, though," said Renee, sitting down at the table. "I tried that already."

Nancy snorted, but it wasn't unkind. "You know how many artists I know 'making a living' from their art? Exactly one—and she's in her 50s, living with her ex-husband because she can't afford to get her own place."

Renee picked up a piece of chalk. "That's pretty much what I thought."

Nancy picked up her water bottle and drank,

leaving a chalk smudge on it. "You don't make art to make a living. You do it because you can't imagine not doing it." She picked up a brown piece of chalk and began drawing a grinning monkey hanging from a tree branch. "I work here part-time, I cover a couple of other stores, and I paint wall murals for private clients. It's better than sitting behind a desk all day—and I still have the energy and inclination to pursue my painting, not to mention buy canvases and brushes and paints." She shrugged. "Everything takes money, even art. Especially art."

Renee watched her drawing, her movements swift and confident. "I've actually done some drawing myself," she said, pushing her chair back. "Could I show you?" She walked to the back and pulled out the chalkboards.

Blank. Blank. Blank. She flipped through them rapidly. "Wait a minute! I know they were back here." She looked up at Nancy. "Are there any more chalkboards, anywhere?"

"That's it."

Renee stopped, looking more closely at the chalkboard she was holding. It had been wiped clean, but she could see faint traces of chalk lines, barely visible ghosts. She knelt down and could make out the forms of her two men and the naked woman of *Luncheon in the Grass*, amid a variety of Dealin' Dave's private label products. "I don't believe this," she said, standing up. "Someone erased them."

Nancy looked over at her.

"Nancy, did you wipe these off?"

She shook her head. "If I'd seen something on there, I would have asked."

Because she gets it, thought Renee. Who else would have access to the chalkboards? And who else would care enough to wipe out her work—before she'd gotten up the nerve to show it to Pam and ask if they could be displayed?

Who else indeed. Renee stomped out of the backroom toward the front of the store. Travis was bagging groceries for a new checker, showing him how to type in a UPC when a bag of apples wouldn't scan.

"Is Pam here?"

"I think she's out on dinner break. Why?" he said.

Renee stopped for a minute, blinking back tears. "You know my signs? She erased them. They're gone."

"What?" He finished bagging the groceries and set them in the shopping cart, thanking the customer. "Kevin, I'll be back. Have Zelieka help you if you have questions."

Travis motioned Renee over to the balloon tank. "Are you sure?"

She crossed her arms over her chest. "Who else would do that? *You* didn't tell her, did you?"

Something crossed over his face. "I may have mentioned that you had some great ideas for new store signage..."

"That's not your job!" Several customers glanced over at them. She lowered her voice. "I wanted to do it when I had all four signs ready." She shook her head fiercely. "And now I can't!" What kind of vindictive, nasty person would do that? Pam had probably been holding her breath, just waiting for Renee to discover them.

"How could you be that stupid? You know she doesn't like me." Renee hated how she sounded, like a spoiled eight-year-old, but she felt like one too. "And besides, who says I need help?"

"Come on." He motioned toward her. "Let's take a walk out back." She followed him out of the store, her arms crossed over her chest. The sky was a brilliant blue, and the alley behind the store was deserted.

"Before you go accusing, are you certain it was her?"

Renee kept her arms crossed. "When did you tell her?"

He tilted his head back, thinking. "Thursday, maybe? No, Friday."

"And the last time I saw them was Thursday, when I finished the fourth one." Renee picked up a piece of gravel and threw it as hard as she could. "I didn't even get to show it to you. It was good."

"I'm sure it was." He hesitated. "Maybe it was Pam."

"Duh!"

"What can I do?" asked Travis. "Forget I said that. What are you going to do?"

Renee shook her head. "I don't know. Is strangling her an option?"

He shook his head.

She sighed. "I don't know. It's not that they're gone. I knew I was working with chalk! We're not talking cave drawings for the ages here."

"True."

"It's the spitefulness of it." Renee started pacing down the length of the alley, then stopped. "It's mean. It's just mean." She turned back to him. "And no one got to see them. I wanted that."

"So why didn't you talk to her about them already?"

"Because I was afraid. Afraid to ask. Afraid that people wouldn't like them."

"Renee, I saw them, and they're tight," he said, using a word she knew he'd picked up from the guys on his cross-country team. "You could redo them, couldn't you?" They continued walking down the alley, the smell of McDonald's fries stronger with each step.

She shrugged. "I could. But I need to figure out how to approach this. No more of this passive-aggressive crap." She pictured Pam's smug face and scowled.

Travis looked around to make sure the alley was empty, and then pulled her toward him. His body was warm and lean, and she let him kiss her briefly.

"I'm still mad."

"At me or her? Or both?"

She thought. "Both of you. But more her," she admitted. She tugged him back toward the store. "Come on. I don't want her to see us out here. She'll just gloat if she knows that she got to me." She lifted her head. "So don't you say anything."

He lifted his hands, palms up. "Absolutely not. I shouldn't have said anything in the first place." He held the door for her as they entered the back room. "Of course had I gotten a 31 on my ACT, I no doubt would have known that, right?"

She couldn't help but laugh, a little. "Probably." Her anger toward him had already faded. She knew he'd been trying to help. Pam was another matter. "No matter what happens with us, you'd better never get back together with her. Am I clear on that?"

He lifted his palms. "I can absolutely, categorically promise you that will never happen."

It still bothered her that he had a past with Pam, but what was she going to do about it? They were both in their 30s, after all. At this point in your life, no one got on the dating plane without baggage of some sort. Everyone had a past. Everyone had prior relationships, heartbreaks, lessons (hopefully) learned. You could say that you didn't want to know about someone's history, but like it or not, you were going to be dealing with that person's history if you got involved with him. "I'll take your word on that."

Later that week, Renee squatted on her hands and knees, dragging her boxes out of her bedroom closet. She carried them out into the tiny living room and sat cross-legged as she opened them.

One box was full of card stock, stamping supplies, bows, buttons, and other found objects she'd occasionally used in her designs. The others held packets of finished cards, notepaper with the names and telephone numbers of card shops and bookstores, and a running list of her expenses and sales.

She picked it up, frowning. She'd thought she'd been so business-like when she'd decided to sell cards for a living, but here was the proof. She'd sold a few cards here and there, but she hadn't done anything more than show up at a few stores and ask them to put her cards on the shelves. She knew enough now about business to realize that wasn't anywhere near enough. She'd need a marketing plan, steady customers, and a product that customers would want to buy.

She pulled out a packet of finished cards, examining them closely. She'd loved the idea of blending art classics with modern day humor, but they hadn't sold all that well. Was it the product? Is this even art? It was her take on art, sure, but what did that matter? Renee sighed, pushing the boxes aside. She'd never be a Manet or a Picasso or a Warhol. She had nothing original to offer. A derivative work would always be derivative.

So why bother. It was clear she couldn't support herself making art, however she defined it. Why do it at all?

She picked up a box lid and a marker and began to doodle. Tiny flowers with little smiling faces, baby rabbits sitting on their haunches, a row of ducks, a castle with turrets and a moat. Drawing was still her first love, but was it enough?

The knock at the door made her jump. "Coming." She pushed herself up and walked through the kitchen to open it.

Travis smelled of wind and sun and sweat. He wore shiny black bicycling shorts, a snug blue, red, and yellow jersey, and leather cycling gloves.

"Hey! I'm finishing up a ride; thought I'd swing by."

"Let's sit out here." She motioned at her miniscule deck.

He sat on the top step, lying back with his lean legs kicked out before him. "Can I get a water?"

Renee had already pulled two bottles of water out of her small fridge, and handed him one.

He opened it and drank half of it in one long pull. "Ahhhhh." He put his head back and shut his eyes.

"How far did you go?"

"'Bout thirty miles. That wind is fierce."

"Or maybe you're getting old."

He shrugged. "Happens to the best of us."

They sat there in the late afternoon sun, not speaking. Travis reached his hand up and stroked her leg with no real intent. "Figure out your next step?"

She took a sip of water. "What, the signs?"

He nodded without looking at her.

"I had a thought about that, actually." Renee watched a squirrel barrel up a nearby tree and perch on a branch, chattering angrily at an unseen assailant. "Can I ask your managerial opinion?"

"Always." He turned his head to look at her.

"What if I go over her head? What if I took it up with Charlene?" Charlene was Dave's district manager who visited the store once or twice a month.

"You serious?"

"If it would work in one store, why not more?"

He considered. "That's bound to piss Pam off."

"Yeah, well, I'm past that." She offered her water bottle to Travis, who had already finished his. "The worst she can say is 'no' and I'm no better off, am I?"

"I suppose not." He sighed and sat up, pulling his legs to his chest. "How will you do it?"

"I already thought of that." Renee had made a list of possible signs, with small illustrations of each. "No point in putting all that time in on more actual signs until I get the go-ahead."

He nodded. "That's smart. And Charlene can think outside the box."

Renee rolled her eyes.

"You know what I mean. She's not the worst person to ask."

Renee stood up. "I heard Pam say she's coming for a store visit Tuesday. Is that right?"

He grinned. "It is. Can I watch?"

Renee shook her head, standing up. "This isn't some kind of revenge. This is a store associate coming in with a smart marketing concept and taking it to the person with the authority to make a decision on behalf of more than one store." She smiled sweetly. "Why shouldn't Dave's benefit from my great idea?"

He stood too, shaking each leg in turn to loosen his muscles. "Who are you, to hide your light under a barrel?"

"It's bushel, actually. 'Don't hide your light under a bushel.'"

He followed her back into the apartment, helping himself to another bottle of water. "That's why I need you around, to correct my poor English usage."

"Is that why?"

He grabbed her waist and pulled her close, the tangy smell of sweat radiating off him. "Among other reasons."

She leaned her body against him, closing her eyes. "What's with the boxes?" he said, stepping into the living room?

She followed. "I don't think I ever told you about my defunct card business."

He sat down on the floor, picking up cards and looking at them, laughing at several. "These are great! Renee, you should sell these."

"Did you hear me? I tried that already."

"And?"

"And I failed."

He sat and looked at her expectantly. "And?"

She sat down on one of the low chairs, tucking one foot underneath her. "They're not original enough."

"How original do they have to be?" He held up the cards. "You've got talent, Renee. You look at the world in a different way than most people. That's what's original." He shook the cards. "Who else could have come up with this idea?"

That was possibly the nicest compliment she'd ever received. She swallowed. "You're saying that because you—well, you know," she finished. "Because we're friends."

"Give me a little credit. We're a bit beyond friends. You're smart enough to figure that out, aren't you?" He leaned forward onto his legs, stretching his back.

She didn't argue with him. "You know what I mean. You can't be objective. Your opinion is tainted. Or at least suspect."

"Screw that. I'd tell you if I thought your work was crap." He looked at her face. "All right. I wouldn't come out and say it was crap. But I wouldn't be praising it if I didn't mean it. I gave up that kind of BS a long time ago."

Renee believed him. "What if I *wanted* you to tell me if it was crap? What if I wanted you to be completely honest? No matter how much it hurt me?"

He thought for a long time, seeming to understand the importance of the question. Finally he came to a decision. "It wouldn't be crap no matter what. Not if you'd done it."

"Don't look for a loophole," she teased.

"Then, yeah I would be honest. If that's what you wanted, then that's what I'd give you," said Travis. "Even if it hurt you." He shook his head. "But I've done that already, and I don't want to do it again."

Renee didn't ask him to promise he wouldn't. That

was an impossible request, and people made promises based on hormones and attraction that didn't outlive a week. The longer they were together—they were kind of together now, weren't they—the more likely he was to hurt her. Or she would hurt him. They'd hurt each other.

Maybe this time, though, she knew more about herself. Maybe her 20s and early 30s had been only a psychic warm-up for what lay ahead. Right now it didn't matter. What did is that she'd taken the big step off of the steep cliff, jumping into the unknown, murky waters below. Choosing to make art was as important--maybe even more important--than the art that resulted, Renee knew. So was choosing to change your life.

Chapter 26
Colleen

A haggle of boys shot by Colleen on the deck, whooping and squirting each other with the water guns specially purchased for the party. "Be careful!" Colleen called automatically before shrugging it off. By day's end, there would no doubt be a fair number of skinned knees, bumped heads, and bruises. Nothing she could do about that, and it was certainly easier than Taylor's parties where the injuries were emotional rather than physical.

But it was worth it. Jordan hadn't wanted a party at Chuck E. Cheese like many of his friends. "I want to have a party in the back yard. Can I, Mommy? Please?"

Colleen envisioned a cadre of screaming five-year-olds tearing apart the yard and running through the house unchecked. "Wouldn't you rather have a party someplace special?" she'd cajoled. "You could have pizza and birthday cake."

Rose's first birthday had been easy enough—a cake for her to dig in, otherwise business as usual. Taylor's wasn't for another month. But Jordan had already been to too many birthday parties not to know what he wanted. He'd insisted, and they'd wound up hosting nine five-year-olds for the afternoon.

Taylor had been allowed to ask a friend—"so I don't

have to play with the babies"—and the two girls had been camped out in her bedroom for several hours, playing with her American Girl dolls. Colleen had been shocked when Taylor had wanted to invite her classmate Jessica instead of Sasha. She hoped it was the beginning of a beautiful preteen friendship.

Colleen looked at her watch. Forty-five more minutes. The cake had been served and the presents opened, Jordan's face leaving no doubt about which gifts he favored.

"All right!" he screamed, tearing off the remaining wrapping paper off the firefighters from the Rescue Heroes series. "This is the exact one I wanted!" He waved it at Colleen and Pete.

"Hi there! Where's the birthday boy?" Renee came walking around the corner of the backyard, followed by the manager Colleen recognized from Dealin' Dave's.

Renee and Colleen hugged. "And you must be Travis. I've seen you at the store."

"I am." He reached over to shake her hand.

Renee looked at the ongoing chaos. "Wow. You are a brave woman."

"Or a crazy one."

Jordan came leaping up the porch two steps at a time, Connor on his heels. He slowed at the top of the steps, carefully stepping around the baby, who was happily shredding left-over wrapping paper. "Mommy! Mommy, it's not over yet, is it?"

Colleen shook her head.

"There's the birthday boy!" Renee knelt and gave him a quick hug. "How old are you again? Eleven? Fifteen? Thirty?"

"I'm FIVE!" He held up his palm, fingers outstretched.

"That's right." Renee handed him the present she'd held behind her back. "This is for my favorite five-year-old."

He tore the package open, pulling out a red basketball jersey. "The Bulls!" It was a tank top, with the team logo and the number 23 on the front.

"Look at the back," said Renee, smiling.

He turned the shirt around and his mouth opened in awe. "It says Jordan!"

"That's right. Because — "

He interrupted. "Because it's Michael Jordan, who was one of the greatest basketball players EVER. And because it's for me! And my name is Jordan!"

Renee stroked his hair. "That's exactly right."

"What do you say?" Colleen prodded.

"Thanks! Thanks a lot!" He grabbed Renee and hugged her, then ran after Monty.

"Nice little boy," said Travis, and Colleen nodded.

"Can I get you something to drink?" She looked over her shoulder for Pete. When she'd told him she needed help with the party, he'd surprised her by creating an elaborate obstacle course for the boys complete with Slip-n-Slides and Super Soakers. Then he'd timed each kid as they completed the course, yelling encouragement. The boys had loved it.

Renee got up. "I'll get something." She trailed her hand over his shoulder as she walked by him, and Colleen saw the look that passed between them. Sex, she thought. Good sex. And maybe something more.

"I hear you're a writer." Travis crossed one ankle over his knee, leaning back in his chair.

Colleen started. "Not really."

"What do you mean? Renee showed me one of your columns from the local paper. The one on walking more, driving less. I thought it was great."

"You did? Thanks." The idea for the column had come to her in a flash. Since the weather had warmed up this spring, she and Jordan and the baby walked the six blocks to Taylor's school to pick her up. She was in the minority—most moms sat, their minivans and SUVs idling, talking on cell phones. But Colleen had come to relish the meandering stroll home, listening to Taylor talk about her school day.

Sometimes Taylor surprised her by offering to push the baby's stroller, or reaching for Colleen's hand. On nice afternoons, Colleen brought a snack and they stopped at the park to swing and slide and run around before they went home. After months of being cooped up indoors, she wanted the kids to have every opportunity to be outside. Choosing to walk meant that things took longer. But that wasn't always a drawback. She felt less rushed, less hurried, than she had before. More "in the moment," as Amelia would say.

"It's still a little strange that people I don't even know are reading what I wrote. I guess I'm not used to it yet."

"Isn't that the attraction, though? You have a voice. And you get to share it."

Colleen grinned, liking him. "You're right. I get to inflict my opinion on complete strangers." But it wasn't that people were reading her words that had changed her. It was that she had something that was hers again, something she alone could claim. Writing had reconnected her with something she'd thought she had lost, a slender strand deep within her that she privately called the essential Colleen. The Colleen she was before the kids. Before Pete. Even before Renee.

Colleen was a mom. She would never stop thinking of herself as a mom. That's the impact a seven-pound, nine-ounce (and an eight-pound, two-ounce, and a seven-pound, fifteen-ounce) human being had on you. But she could admit now that she'd wanted more than that. Or at least something extra. She'd tried to swamp that desire with guilt, ease it with alcohol, and distract it with mindless magazine stories. Nothing had worked until she'd acknowledged it, listened to it, and finally honored it.

That was what Amelia would call moving with the world, not against it. It was what Renee would call progress. Colleen simply called it peace.

***

About the Author

Kelly James-Enger is an author and ghostwriter who lives in a Chicago suburb very much like the one in this book. She shares her home with one husband, one son, one daughter, and one golden retriever. Author of more than a dozen published nonfiction books, *The Honesty Index* is her third novel. Her first two novels, **Did you Get the Vibe?**, and **White Bikini Panties**, are currently available as e-books.

In addition to writing fiction, Kelly is the author of more than a dozen published books including **Writer for Hire: 101 Secrets to Freelance Success** (Writer's Digest Books, 2012), and has a popular blog on freelance writing, **http://dollarsanddeadlines.blogspot.com**. You can reach her through her website, **www.becomebodywise.com**, or email her at **Kelly@becomebodywise.com**.

www.ingramcontent.com/pod-product-compliance
Lightning Source LLC
Chambersburg PA
CBHW051458170626
46811CB00002B/542